THE ILLUSTRATED
STORY OF
O

THE ILLUSTRATED STORY OF O

PHOTOGRAPHS BY DORIS KLOSTER

With extracts from the original text by Pauline Réage

Palast Verlag GmbH
Frankenstraße 174
50374 Erftstadt
Germany
www.palast-verlag.de

All rights reserved!

ISBN: 978-3-939527-11-4

Edition 2012

By courtesy of
Eddison Sadd Editions
PO BOX 583
Maids Moreton
Buckingham, MK18 1TG
Great Britain

Text extracts from *Histoire d'O* by Pauline Réage copyright © Société Nouvelle des Éditions Pauvert 1979
English translation by Sabine D'Estrée copyright © Grove Press, Inc. 1965
Introduction copyright © Jean-Jacques Pauvert 2000
Photographs and Preface copyright © Doris Kloster 2000
Copyright of the original edition © Eddison Sadd Editions 2000

The right of Doris Kloster to be identified as the author of this work has been asserted by her in
accordance with the Copyright, Designs and Patents Act 1988.

No part of this book may be used or reproduced in any manner whatsoever without written permission
except in the case of brief quotations embodied in critical articles or reviews.

Coverdesign by agilmedien gbr, Niederkassel, Germany
Printed and bound by Drogowiec-Pl, Kielce, Poland

CONTENTS

PREFACE 7

by Doris Kloster

INTRODUCTION 11

by Jean-Jacques Pauvert

THE ILLUSTRATED STORY OF O 17

Photographs by Doris Kloster

With extracts from the original text by Pauline Réage

ACKNOWLEDGMENTS 120

PREFACE

by Doris Kloster

Since its publication in 1954 in Paris, Story of O by Pauline Réage has never been out of print. This popular and psychologically profound work of erotic literature caused a sensation when it was released, and it still has the power to disgust and shock timid readers. It is a book that relates potent, forbidden fantasies that, even today, few people dare to think, speak of, or write.

The story involves a young, beautiful fashion photographer, O, who lives in Paris. As the novel opens, her lover, René, takes her to a château in Roissy. Here O is introduced into a world where women are subjugated, physically abused and turned into sexual slaves. O submits to René's wishes that she be imprisoned, whipped and made completely available to the desires of other men. After taking her from the château, René introduces O to Sir Stephen, a more severe and experienced sadist. Sir Stephen, in turn, passes O into the hands of Anne-Marie, the ruler over a household of naked women. And at every step in this systematic degradation, O finds deeper and deeper levels of sexual and psychological satisfaction. Near the end of the novel O wonders, "Would she ever dare to tell him that no pleasure, no joy, no figment of her imagination could ever compete with the happiness she felt at the way he used her with such utter freedom, at the notion that he could do anything with her, that there was no limit, no restriction in the manner with which, on her body, he might search for pleasure?"

The author, whose real name was Dominique Aury, created Story of O as a way to hold the interest of her long-time lover, critic and intellectual, Jean Paulhan. When Aury suggested she could write in a style that would impress and excite the man she feared might leave her, he expressed skepticism. Therefore Story of O is, on several levels, a *woman's successful response to a man's challenge. When asked on one occasion, "aren't these male fantasies?", Aury said, "I don't know, all I can say is that they are honest fantasies."*

Paulhan championed his lover's Story of O *among literary scholars, and wrote the preface for the work. It was he who found the book's publisher: after the manuscript had been turned down by a number of other editors, Paulhan brought the work to Jean-Jacques Pauvert, a daring young publisher who had previously published the entire works of the Marquis de Sade. I am honored that Jean-Jacques has written the introduction for this illustrated version of* Story of O.

While my work in previous photo books have tended to be documentary in style, dealing with real life and real individuals, this book revels in pure fantasy. Creating the photographic representation of the most famous work in erotica has been a long-standing dream of mine. Story of O *is both an esteemed work of literature and a primer in alternative sexuality. I considered the task of realizing* Story of O *in pictures a challenge and a great responsibility. I wanted to portray in detail the intense eroticism of the novel, yet somehow not restrict the vision brought by the story into the mind's eye of its myriad admirers throughout the world. It is appropriate that a woman undertook the visualization of this novel, written by a woman. The character, O, is herself a photographer; and she is not simply submissive. Especially in her relationships with other women in the story, she often proves to be wilful and manipulative.*

To me, Story of O *is a timeless literary work, not a historical artifact. Therefore, this book of photographs does not attempt to recreate the original story in every detail. However, I did try, whenever possible, to match the characters, clothing, props and settings to the descriptions in the novel. I wanted to photograph the story in locations that evoke the mystery and fantasy that is the* Story of O. *The novel is set in Paris and its environs, the most romantic locale in the world, and the home of the Marquis de Sade.*

Generations of artists have sought inspiration within the demi-monde of this great city. Degas, Toulouse-Lautrec, Manet, Zola and many others have come here and portrayed their fantasies of sexually available women. To infuse this book with romance and authenticity, I brought my models, crew and equipment to a number of settings in Paris, including the national monument and castle on the Île de la Cité, the Conciergerie, and châteaux in the Loire Valley, including the seventeeth-century fortress, Château de Saint-Loup.

In his preface to Story of O, *Jean Paulhan writes that the book is dangerous because it marks the reader, and "leaves him not quite, or not at all, the same as he was before he read it." That was certainly the case for me, for I never had the same perceptions of sexuality after having read* Story of O. *The work rekindled deep and potent fantasies from a time when early glimmers of sexuality appeared to me only in dreams. I hope that by experiencing* Story of O *in a new way, through my book, readers may find new pathways where their imagination and memory can discover fresh resonances with Aury's vision.*

Doris Kloster
Paris, April 2000

INTRODUCTION

by Jean-Jaques Pauvert

The publication of Story of O *was one of those rare adventures in publishing, paradoxically both disappointing and exhilarating. It cannot be summed up in one date— the publication date—but instead covers a period of over two decades.*

Story of O came out in June 1954 as the work of an author named Pauline Réage, with a preface by Jean Paulhan. It was a time when freedom of expression, a precious tradition in France, was at its lowest ebb. Court proceedings taken against me in 1947 over the publication of the Marquis de Sade were dragging on, due to newly passed hypocritical laws that accumulated charges.

I had been so enthralled by the manuscript of Pauline Réage, however, that I had inserted a little pamphlet in the book which claimed: "We guarantee that Story of O *will mark a date in the history of all literature."*

I was 28 years old, and although not without professional experience (I had published my first book at 19), it would be fair to say that I was still somewhat naïve. Actually, I was convinced that Story of O *was going to revolutionize the book trade, that I would sell hundreds of thousands of copies across the world, and that moral attitudes would change overnight. The audacity of this novel seemed to me to be liberating rather than provocative. I perceived the promise of a new freedom. And I expected to cause a shock.*

As things turned out the shock, if anything at all, was more of a dull thud and remained almost totally unnoticed.

Only three reviews appeared in the press—albeit two of them very significant. The third one, published first, consisted of a short article in a weekly called Dimanche matin—*now extinct—by Claude Elsen (author of* Homo eroticus *published by Gallimard).*

"All in all," wrote Claude Elsen, "far fom belonging to the licentious genre, Story of O *is close to those legends or those epic poems which celebrate* l'amour fou, *or the 'Song of Songs', or the romance of Tristan and Isolde"…*

This was quite a good start. But in the Nouvelle Revue française *of 1 May 1955, Georges Bataille went further:*

"…The eroticism found in Story of O *also contains the impossible aspect of eroticism. To accept eroticism means to accept the impossible—or more to the point, to accept that desiring the impossible constitutes eroticism. O's paradox is similar to that of the visionary who dies of not dying, or to martyrdom that consists of compassion shown by the torturer to the victim. This book reaches beyond the word, breaks out of its own bonds, dispels any fascination for eroticism by revealing the greater fascination exerted by the impossible. What is impossible here is not only death, but total and absolute solitude…"*

A month later Critique, *a confidential but influential magazine, published a review by André Pieyre de Mandiargues. It was as long as Bataille's article. Under the superb heading, "Irons, fire and darkness in the soul", Pieyre de Mandiargues pointed out that "this novel, which is anything but vulgar, appears to borrow from publications generally classified as crudely pornographic. This may seem surprising, yet the author is right. For did not Julien Gracq state, in his preface to* Au Château d'Argol, *that the outcome of all battles, whether victory or defeat, is determined by identical tactics? In his own work, Gracq deliberately restricted his instruments of terror to the kind found in the Gothic novels of the late eighteenth and early nineteenth centuries. Similarly, Réage exploits the well-tried recipes used in the hundred or more clandestine books distributed under the counter. … And when an author like Réage—who, as I said earlier, constructs a story with the art of a very great writer—chooses to dispense with any fantasy in the details, it is safe to assume that she does so out of pride, because she aims to excel using only ordinary means…"*

However, in spite of recommendations from those two great names (as well as from Jean Paulhan), the few who read Story of O *reacted in a way that was, for me, totally unexpected. Of course, it must be said that neither the* Journal du dimanche, *nor the* Nouvelle Revue française, *nor* Critique, *were very widely read. Furthermore, in the context of the times, these people, who were well-informed, could have but one reaction: they were terrified.*

In short, what I had failed to realize was that the book trade was not ready to handle this kind of literature. Everybody was talking about Bonjour tristesse, *by Françoise Sagan, a novel which had come out at the same time and was regarded as scandalous. But there was no mention of* Story of O *anywhere, except by word-of-mouth. Booksellers who had shown some interest in the book were unanimous: it would be banned.*

Indeed, the police was getting nervous. Story of O *had been the subject of an inquiry by one of the book (censorship) commissions set up by the Department of the Interior. The ruling of the commission was unequivocal:*

"After hearing the report of Mr. … and having duly considered the matter:

"In view of the fact that this book, published by Jean-Jacques Pauvert, relates the adventures of a young woman who, in order to please her lover, submits to every erotic whim and ill-treatment

"In view of the fact that this book is violently and consciously immoral, that it contains scenes of debauch between two or more people, as well as scenes of sexual abuse, and contains a seedbed of abhorrent and reprehensible behavior, thereby constituting an outrage to public decency

"The commission concludes that proceedings should be taken against it."

As it happened, no proceedings were taken. I was interrogated, but preserved the author's anonymity, while Jean Paulhan delighted in confusing the police with improbable leads. Moreover, pressure from mysterious quarters was brought to bear in favour of the work.

Booksellers were nonetheless afraid, and less than 2,000 copies of Story of O *were sold in its first year.*

On the other hand, it turned out that during that year each copy was read by at least ten to twenty people. Story of O *was passed discreetly from hand to hand. The book was pursuing its career underground, and sales rose every month. Some years later, the author of* Emmanuelle *pointed to the profound impact* Story of O *had made:*

"It is often said of someone who has experienced a certain event that 'he or she was never the same again'. Well, this novel was precisely such an event in our lives. It has transformed us. We are marked by it, more lastingly and more deeply than the red-hot irons branded O, who bears the stigmas in our name... Without Story of O, Emmanuelle *may never have been born."*

And so it was that I watched Story of O's *progress, year after year, silently winning over a thousand, two thousand, ten thousand new readers. The "sexual revolution" of the late 60s brought it to the summit of its success. In the United States, thanks to Barney Rossett, Publisher at Grove Press, it was an instant best seller. Little by little,* Story of O *became the most widely translated French novel in the world—just as I had predicted twenty years earlier. I had simply spoken too soon.*

Finally, in 1975, Story of O *was made into a film (the French weekly,* L'Express, *produced a memorable front cover to mark the occasion), consecrating the triumph of a book which, by then, had sold millions of copies.*

To conclude, we must speak of the author, since the very fact that she was a woman—or was she?—has been for a long time the source of heated debate.

Two camps were irreconcilably opposed: on one side stood those who were absolutely certain from the first that the novel had been written by a woman; on the other, those who could not—and still cannot—bring themselves to accept that no man ever had a hand in it.

We know now, and have done for some time, that the woman who described how, "one evening … , instead of picking up a book before going to sleep, she curled up on her left side and, with a strong black pencil in her right hand [started on] the story she had promised to write", was Dominique Aury, Editorial Secretary at the Nouvelle Revue française. *And that she had worked practically on her own.*

What matters most is that Story of O *was written by a woman. There is no need for me to elaborate on the consequences. They were many and varied. For better or for worse.*

What matters to me, today, is that this novel has preserved its suggestive powers intact to the point of inspiring a young woman of the new millennium to express her own fantasies.

Doris Kloster, whose unique talent lies in her subtle treatment of any subject, has worked hard, meticulously sticking to the text, to explore her own vision of Story of O *through her art. Of course, being more practised in the literary than in the visual medium, I cannot presume to judge of the result. But I can attest to the extraordinary conscientiousness she showed in her endeavour to recreate a fantasy through her photography.*

In what new light will the Story of O, *with its newly acquired dimension, be perceived by the present generations? We long to see.*

But the fact that, almost fifty years on, Doris Kloster should have chosen Story of O *to attend her on this vital journey into herself, proves that perhaps I was not altogether wrong, one day in 1954.*

Jean-Jacques Pauvert
Paris, April 2000

THE ILLUSTRATED
STORY OF O

PHOTOGRAPHS BY DORIS KLOSTER

With extracts from the original text by Pauline Réage

THE TEXT EXTRACTS

The text accompanying the photographs has been selected from *Story of O* as written by
Pauline Réage. It was originally published as *Histoire d'O* by Jean-Jacques Pauvert
in Paris in 1954, and translated from the French by Sabine d'Estrée for the Grove Press
edition copyright © 1965 by Grove Press, Inc. It is reproduced by permission of
Société Nouvelle des Éditions Pauvert, Paris.

THE CHARACTERS

Story of O relates the experiences of a young Parisian fashion photographer, **O**.
Her lover **René** admits her to a secret community at Roissy dedicated to sexual excesses.
Her love for René enables her to bear the extreme attentions of her lover and others.
On her release she is introduced by René to his half-brother **Sir Stephen**, an English
aristocrat. With René's agreement, Sir Stephen asks O to become his sexual slave, and
again O's love for René enables her to accept. O photographs **Jacqueline**, a model,
and René and Sir Stephen ask O to lure her to Roissy. Sir Stephen takes O to meet
Anne-Marie, a dominatrix who arranges for O to be pierced to carry two iron rings
bearing Sir Stephen's initials. Later, O is branded. The novel concludes with a ball in the
south of France hosted by Sir Stephen's friend, the Commander, a member of the Roissy
community, during which O enters in dramatic fashion wearing an owl mask,
lead on a chain by **Natalie**, Jacqueline's younger sister.

. . . it was the unknown friend who explained to the young woman that her lover had been entrusted with the task of getting her ready, that he was going to tie her hands behind her back, unfasten her stockings and roll them down, remove her garter belt, her panties, and her brassiere, and blindfold her. That she would then be turned over to the château, where in due course she would be instructed as to what she should do.

And, in fact, as soon as she had been thus undressed and bound, they helped her to alight from the car after a trip that lasted half an hour, guided her up a few steps and, with her blindfold still on, through one or two doors. . . .

. . . The door had been opened by two women, two young and beautiful women dressed in the garb of pretty eighteenth-century chambermaids: full skirts made out of some light material, which were long enough to conceal their feet; tight bodices, laced or hooked in front, which sharply accentuated the bust line; lace frills around the neck; half-length sleeves. They were wearing eye shadow and lipstick. Both wore a close-fitting collar and had tight bracelets on their wrists.

I know it was at this point that they freed O's hands, which were still tied behind her back, and told her to get undressed, they were going to bathe her and make her up. They proceeded to strip her till she hadn't a stitch of clothing left, then put her clothes away neatly in one of the closets. She was not allowed to bathe herself, and they did her hair as at the hairdresser's, making her sit in one of those large chairs which tilts back . . .

. . . she was seated on this chair, naked, and they kept her from either crossing her legs or bringing them together. And since the wall in front of her was covered from floor to ceiling with a large mirror, which was unbroken by any shelving, she could see herself, thus open, each time her gaze strayed to the mirror.

When she was properly made up and prepared—her eyelids penciled lightly; her lips bright red; the tip and halo of her breasts highlighted with pink; the edges of her nether lips rouged; her armpits and pubis generously perfumed, and perfume also applied to the furrow between her thighs, the furrow beneath her breasts, and to the hollows of her hands—she was led into a room where a three-sided mirror, and another mirror behind, enabled her to examine herself closely. She was told to sit down on the ottoman, which was set between the mirrors, and wait. . . .

... when the two women returned, one was carrying a dressmaker's tape measure and the other a basket. With them came a man dressed in a long purple robe, the sleeves of which were gathered at the wrists and full at the shoulders. When he walked the robe flared open, from the waist down. One could see that beneath his robe he had on some sort of tights which covered his legs and thighs but left the sex exposed. It was the sex that O saw first, when he took his first step, then the whip, made of leather thongs, which he had stuck in his belt. Then she saw that the man was masked by a black hood—which concealed even his eyes behind a network of black gauze—and, finally, that he was also wearing fine black kid gloves.

Using the familiar *tu* form of address, he told her not to move and ordered the women to hurry. The woman with the tape then took the measurements of O's neck and wrists. Though on the small side, her measurements were in no way out of the ordinary, and it was easy enough to find the right-sized collar and bracelets, in the basket the other woman was carrying. ...

... they fastened the two bracelet rings together behind her back. They attached a long red cape to the ring of her collar and draped it over her shoulders. It covered her completely, but opened when she walked, since, with her hands behind her back, she had no way of keeping it closed. One woman preceded her, opening the doors, and the other followed, closing them behind her. They crossed a vestibule, two drawing rooms, and went into the library where four men were having coffee. They were wearing the same long robes as the first, but no masks ...

33

. . . O was blindfolded again. Then they made her walk forward—she stumbled slightly as she went—until she felt that she was standing in front of the fire around which the four men were seated: she could feel the heat, and in the silence she could hear the quiet crackling of the burning logs. She was facing the fire. Two hands lifted her cape, two others—after having checked to see that her bracelets were attached—descended the length of her back and buttocks. The hands were not gloved, and one of them penetrated her in both places at once, so abruptly that she cried out. Someone laughed. Someone else said:

"Turn her around, so we can see the breasts and the belly."

They turned her around, and the heat of the fire was against her back. A hand seized one of her breasts, a mouth fastened on the tip of the other. But suddenly she lost her balance and fell backward (supported by whose arms?), while they opened her legs and gently spread her lips. Hair grazed the insides of her thighs. She heard them saying that they would have to make her kneel down. This they did. She was extremely uncomfortable in this position, especially because they forbade her to bring her knees together and because her arms pinioned behind her forced her to lean forward.

Then they let her rock back a bit, so that she was half-sitting on her heels, as nuns are wont to do.

"You've never tied her up?"

"No, never."

"And never whipped her either?"

"No, never whipped her either. But as a matter of fact . . ."

It was her lover speaking.

"As a matter of fact," the other voice went on, "if you do tie her up from time to time, or whip her just a little, and she begins to like it, that's no good either. You have to get past the pleasure stage, until you reach the stage of tears."

Then they made O get up and were on the verge of untying her, probably in order to attach her to some pole or wall, when someone protested that he wanted to take her first, right there on the spot. So they made her kneel down again, this time with her bust on an ottoman, her hands still tied behind her, with her hips higher than her torso. Then one of the men, holding her with both his hands on her hips, plunged into her belly. He yielded to a second. The third wanted to force his way into the narrower passage and, driving hard, made her scream. When he let her go, sobbing and befouled by tears beneath her blindfold, she slipped to the floor, only to feel someone's knees against her face, and she realized that her mouth was not to be spared. . . .

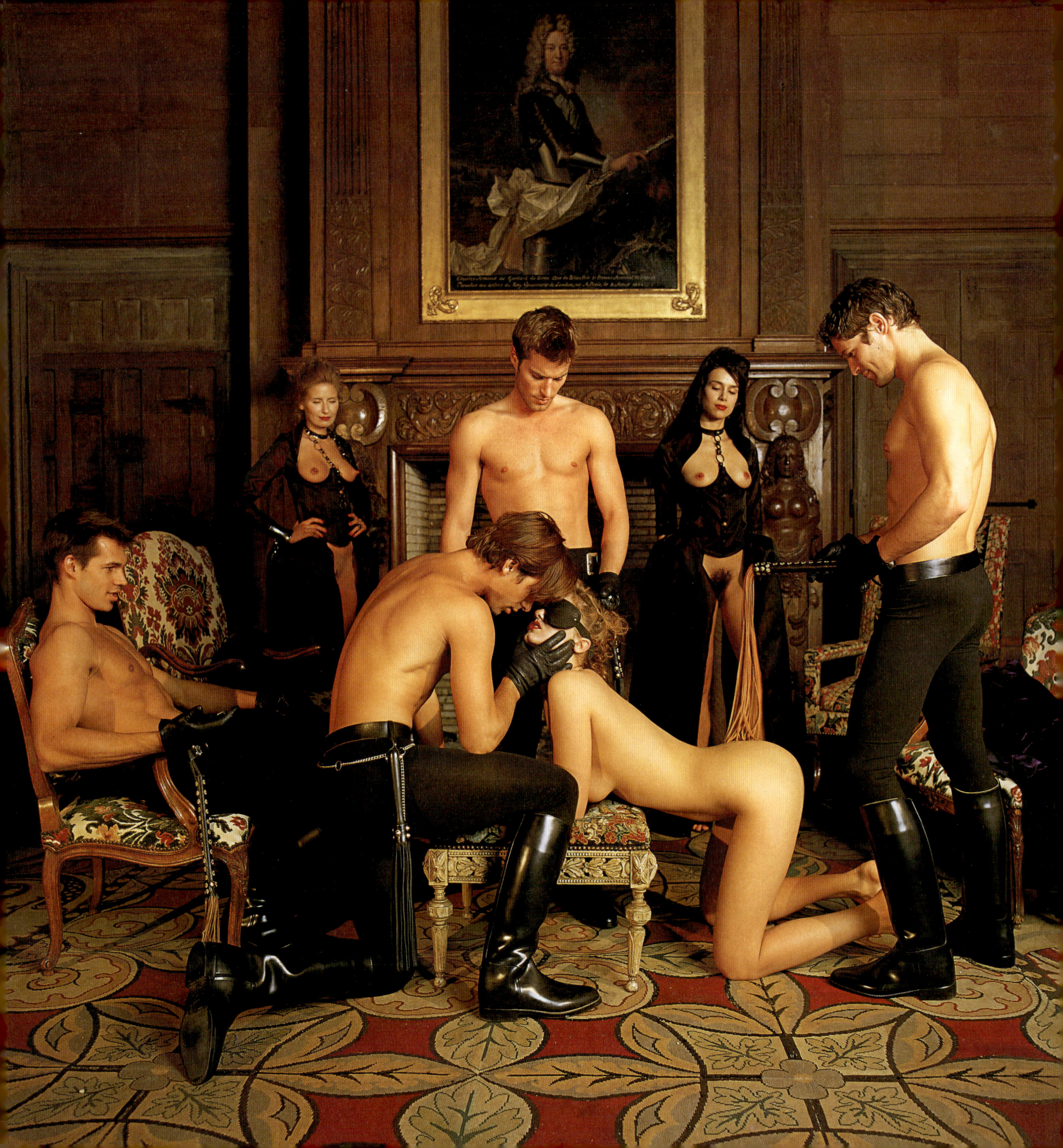

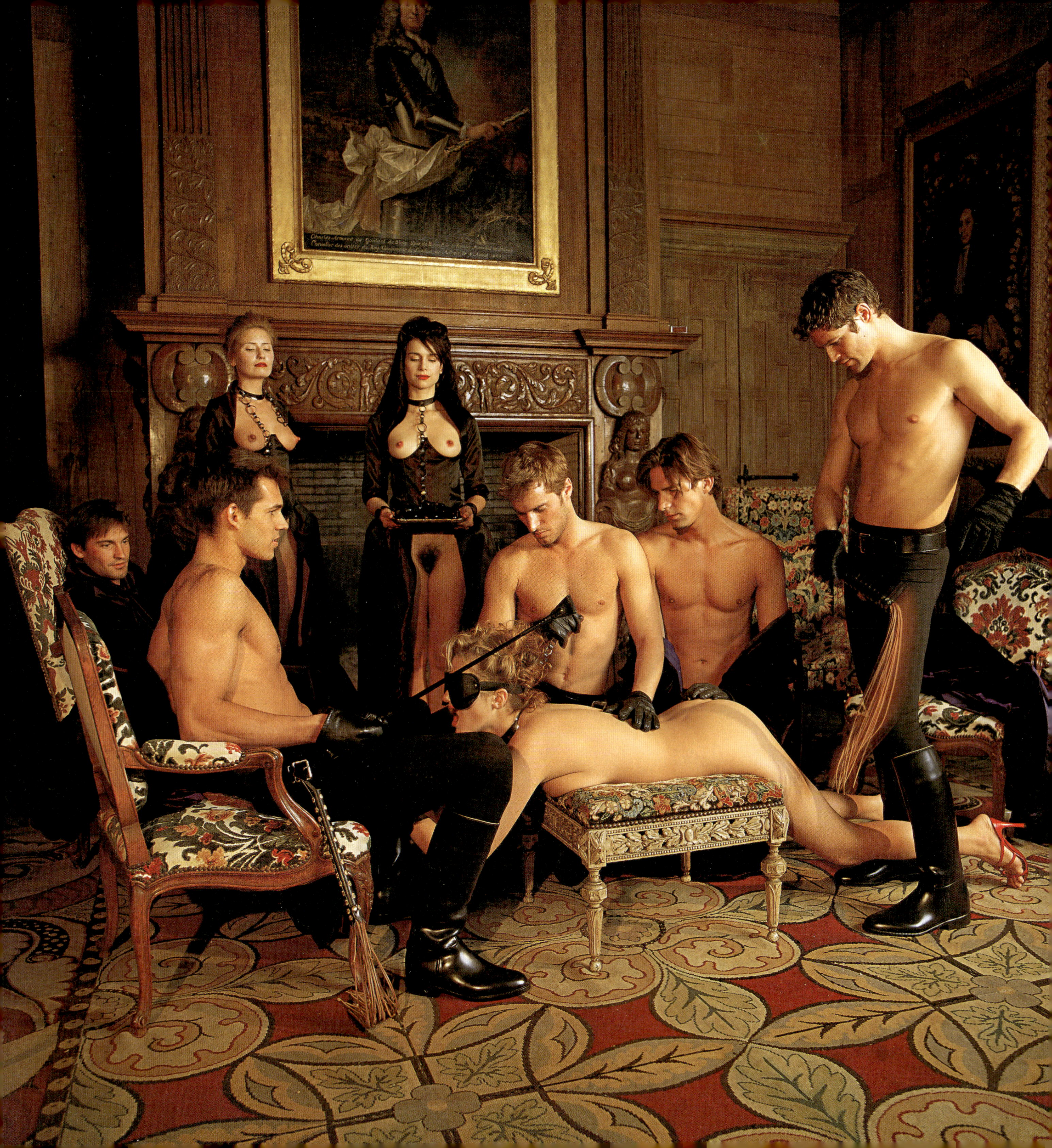

. . . All of a sudden they removed her blindfold. The large room, the walls of which were lined with bookcases, was dimly lit by a single wall lamp and by the light of the fire, which was beginning to burn more brightly. Two of the men were standing and smoking. Another was seated, a riding crop on his knees, and the one leaning over her fondling her breast was her lover. All four of them had taken her, and she had not been able to distinguish him from the others.

They explained to her that this was how it would always be, as long as she was in the château, that she would see the faces of those who violated or tormented her, but never at night, and she would never know which ones had been responsible for the worst. The same would be true when she was whipped, except that they wanted her to see herself being whipped, and so this once she would not be blindfolded. They, on the other hand, would don their masks, and she would not longer be able to tell them apart. . . .

42

. . . Her hands were still behind her back. They showed her the riding crop, which was long, black, and delicate, made of thin bamboo encased in leather, the kind one sees in the windows of better riding equipment shops; the leather whip, which the first man she had seen had been carrying in his belt, was long and consisted of six lashes knotted at the end. There was a third whip of fairly thin cords, each with several knots at the end: the cords were quite stiff, as though they had been soaked in water, which in fact they had, as O discovered, for they caressed her belly with them and nudged open her thighs; so that she could feel how stiff and damp the cords were against the tender, inner skin. Then there were the keys and the steel chains on the console table. . . .

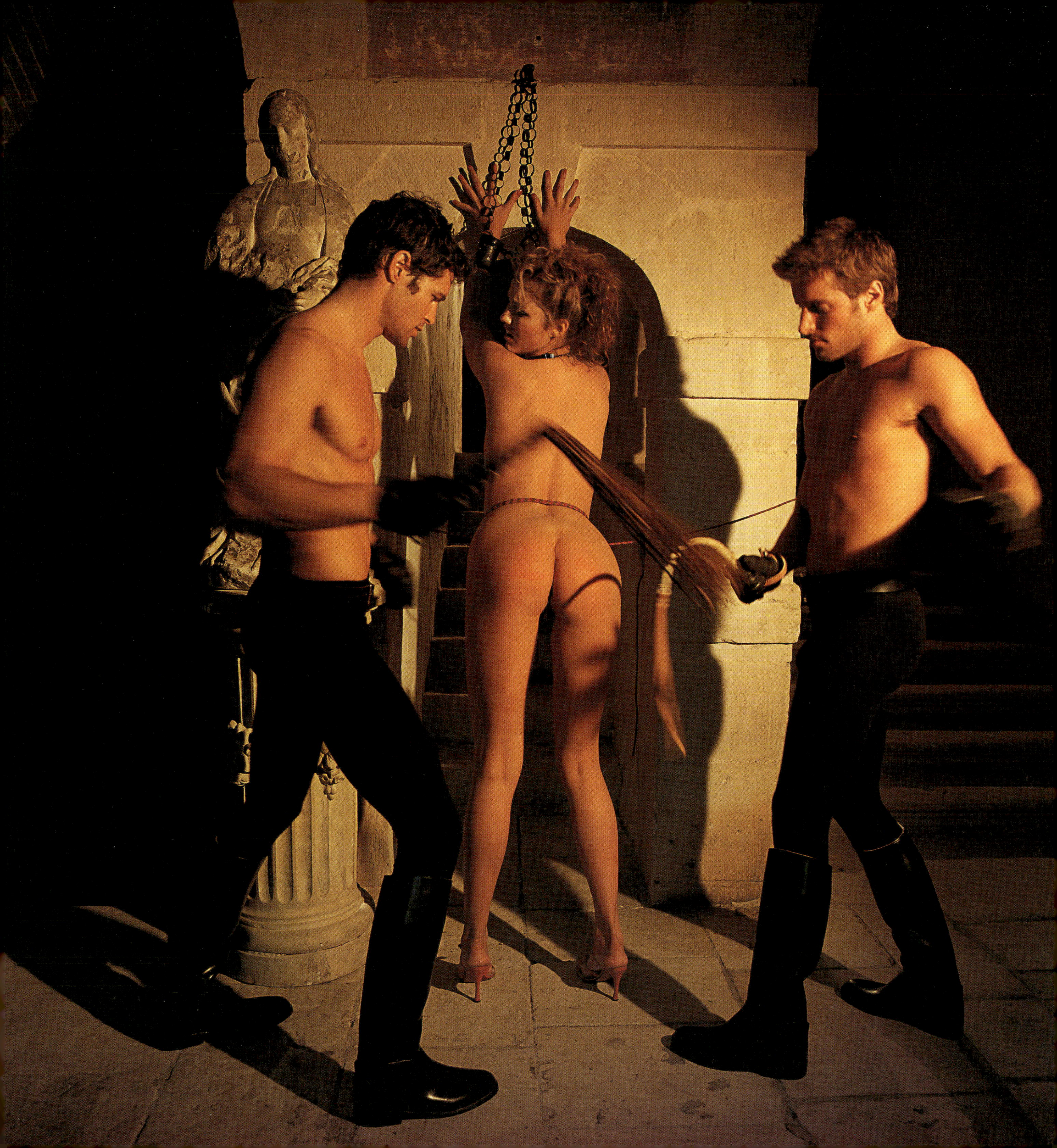

... They said that, with the exception of her hands, which would be held just above her head, she would thus be able to move and see the blows coming: that in principle she would be whipped only on the thighs and buttocks, in other words between her waist and knees, in the same region which had been prepared in the car that had brought her here, when she had been made to sit naked on the seat, but that in all likelihood one of the four men present would want to mark her thighs with the riding crop, which makes lovely long deep welts which last a long time. She would not have to endure all this at once; there would be ample time for her to scream, to struggle, and to cry. They would grant her some respite, but as soon as she had caught her breath they would start in again, judging the results not from her screams or tears but from the size and color of the welts they had raised. ...

. . . When O was dressed and resettled in her chair beside the fire, her pallor accentuated by the color of the dress, the two young women, who had not uttered a word, prepared to leave. One of the four friends seized one of them as she passed, made a sign for the other to wait, and brought the girl he had stopped back toward O. He turned her around and, holding her by the waist with one hand, lifted her skirt with the other, in order to demonstrate to O, he said, the practical advantages of the costume and show how well designed it was. . . .

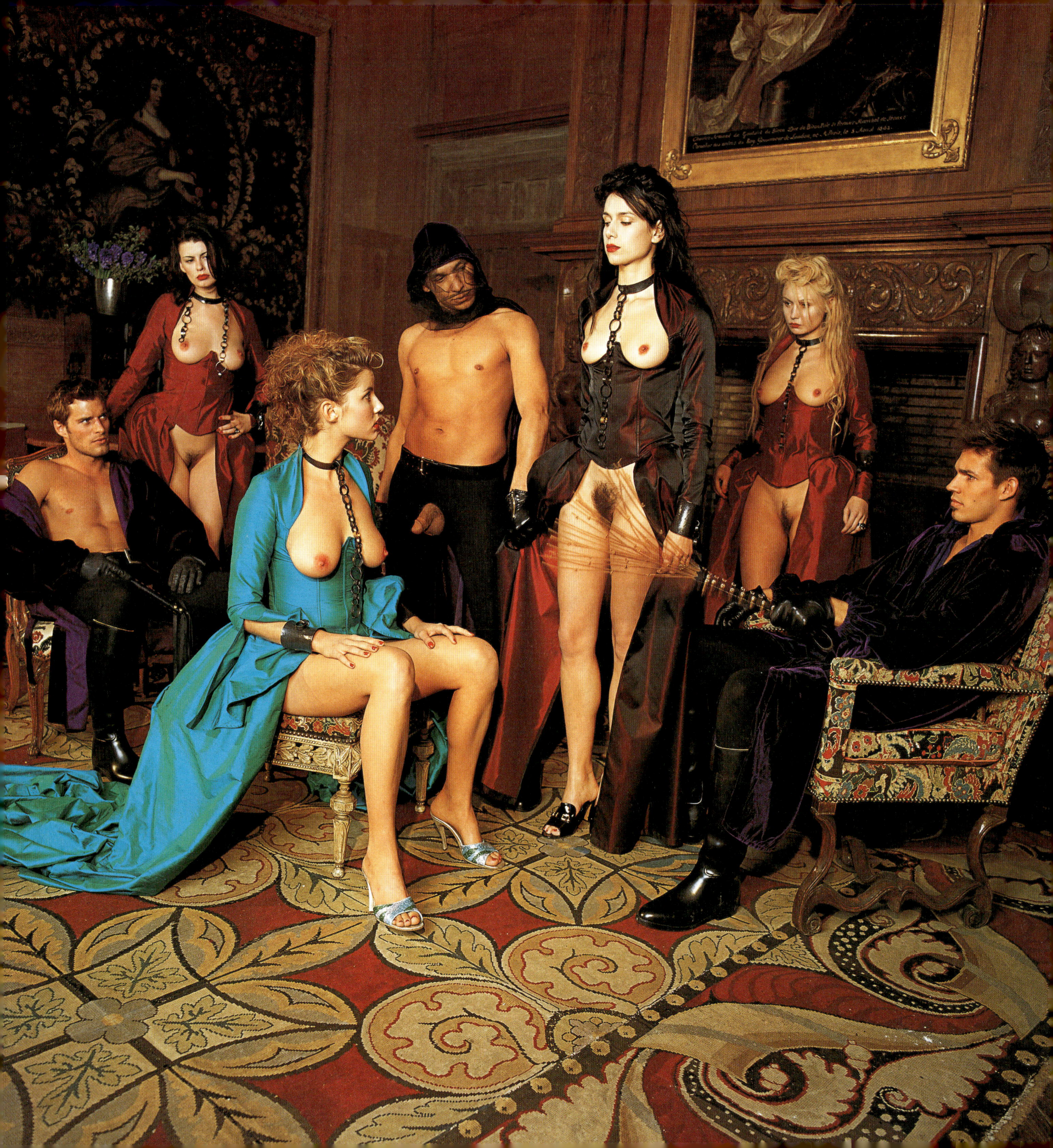

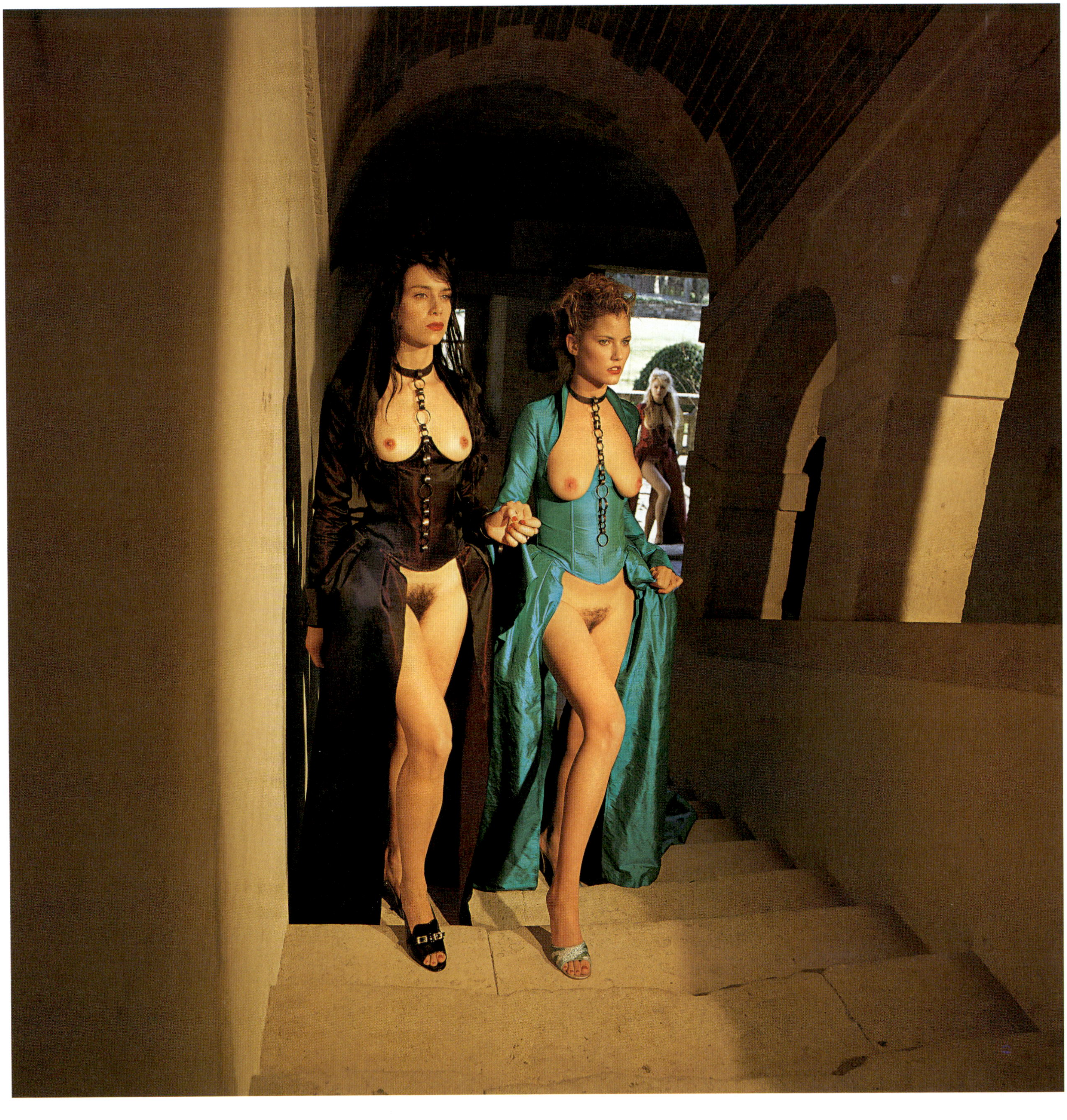

. . . The mules banged on the red tiles of the hallway, where doors succeeded doors, discreet and clean, with tiny locks, like the doors of the rooms in big hotels. O was working up the courage to ask whether each of these rooms was occupied, and by whom, when one of her companions, whose voice she had not yet heard, said to her:

"You're in the red wing, and your valet's name is Pierre."

"What valet?" said O, struck by the gentleness of the voice. "And what's your name?"

"Andrée."

"Mine is Jeanne," said the second.

"The valet is the one who has the keys," the first one went on, "the one who will chain and unchain you, who will whip you when you are to be punished and when the others have no time for you." . . .

50

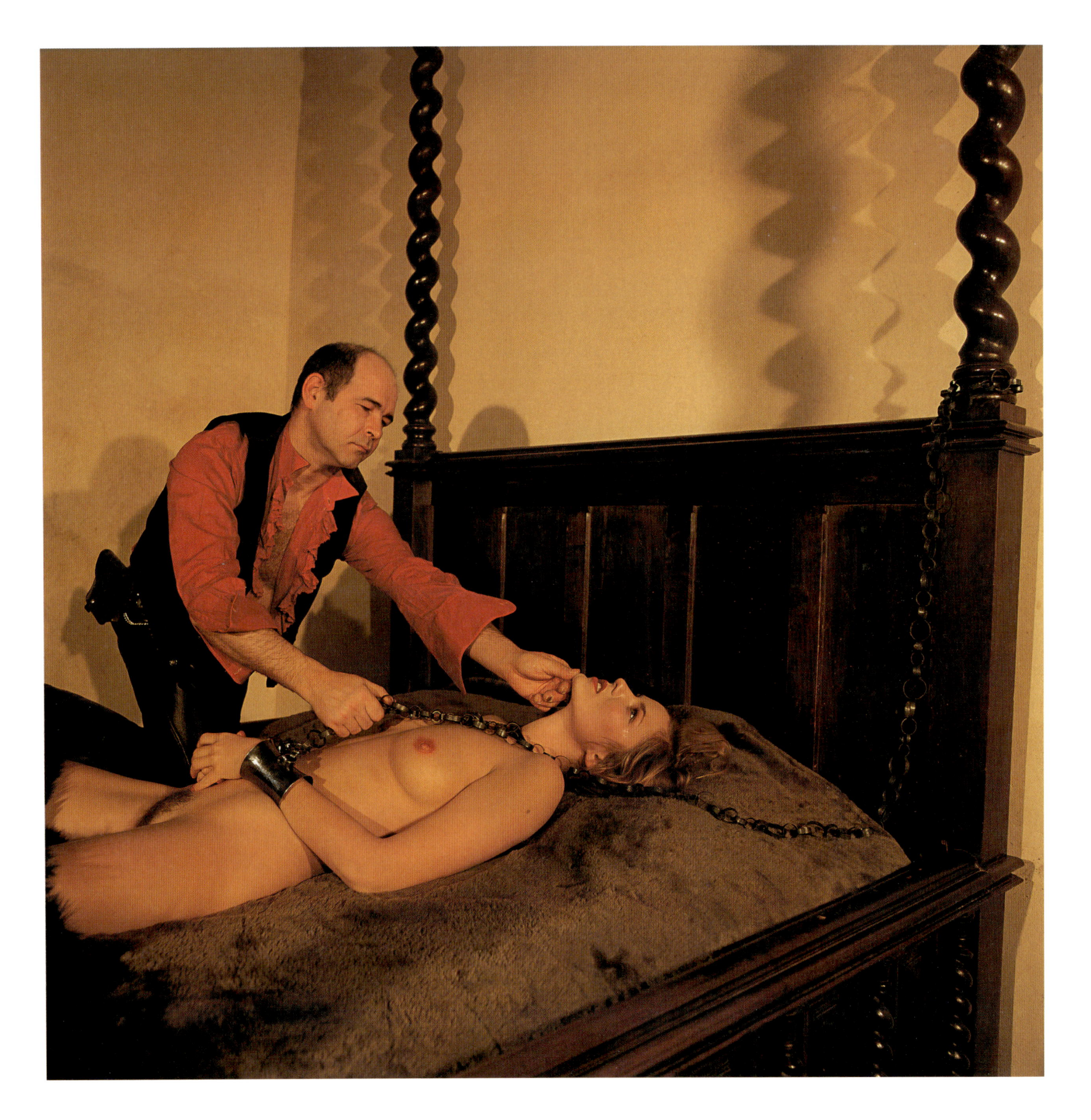

. . . "Behold the lovely lady," said the valet as he entered. And he seized both her hands. He slipped one of the bracelet hooks into the other, so that her wrists were tightly joined, then clipped both these hooks to the ring of the necklace. Thus her hands were joined as in an attitude of prayer, at the level of her neck. All that remained to be done was to chain her to the wall with the chain that was lying on the bed and was attached to the ring above. He unfastened the hook by which the other end was attached and pulled on it in order to shorten it. O was forced to move to the head of the bed, where he made her lie down. The chain clicked in the ring, and was so tight that the young woman could do no more than move from one side of the bed to the other or stand up on either side of the headboard. . . .

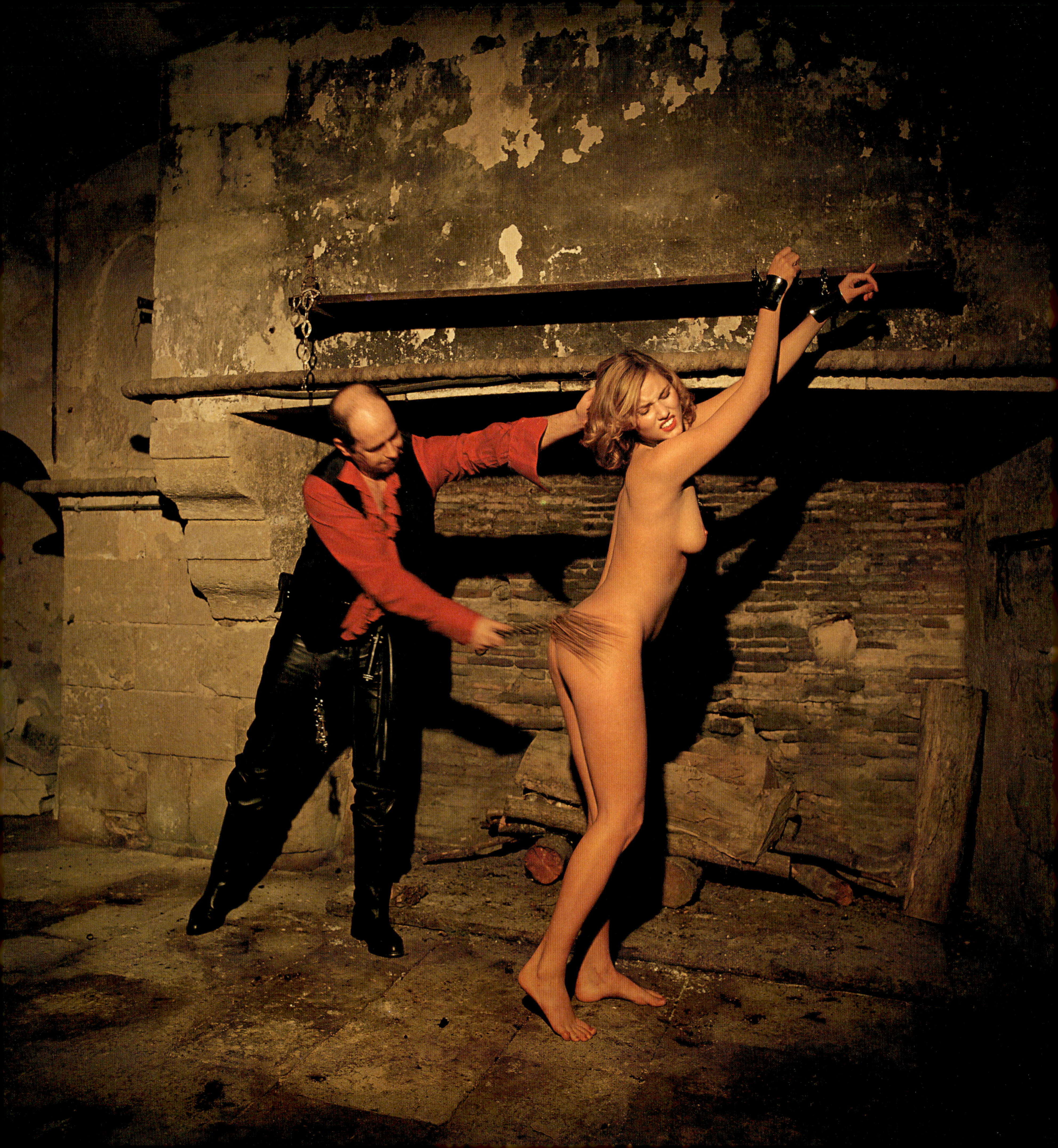

. . . At the same time as she heard a whistling noise in the semi-darkness O felt a terrible burning across her back, and she screamed. Pierre flogged her with all his might. He did not wait for her screams to subside, but struck her again four times, being careful each time to lash her above or below the preceding spot, so that the traces would be all the clearer. Even after he had stopped she went on screaming, and the tears streamed down into her open mouth.

"Please be good enough to turn around," he said, and since she, who was completely distracted, failed to obey, he took her by the hips without letting go of his riding crop, the handle of which brushed against her waist. When she was facing him, he moved back slightly and lowered his crop on the front of her thighs as hard as he could. The whole thing had lasted five minutes. When he had left, after having turned out the light and closed the bathroom door, O was left moaning in the darkness . . .

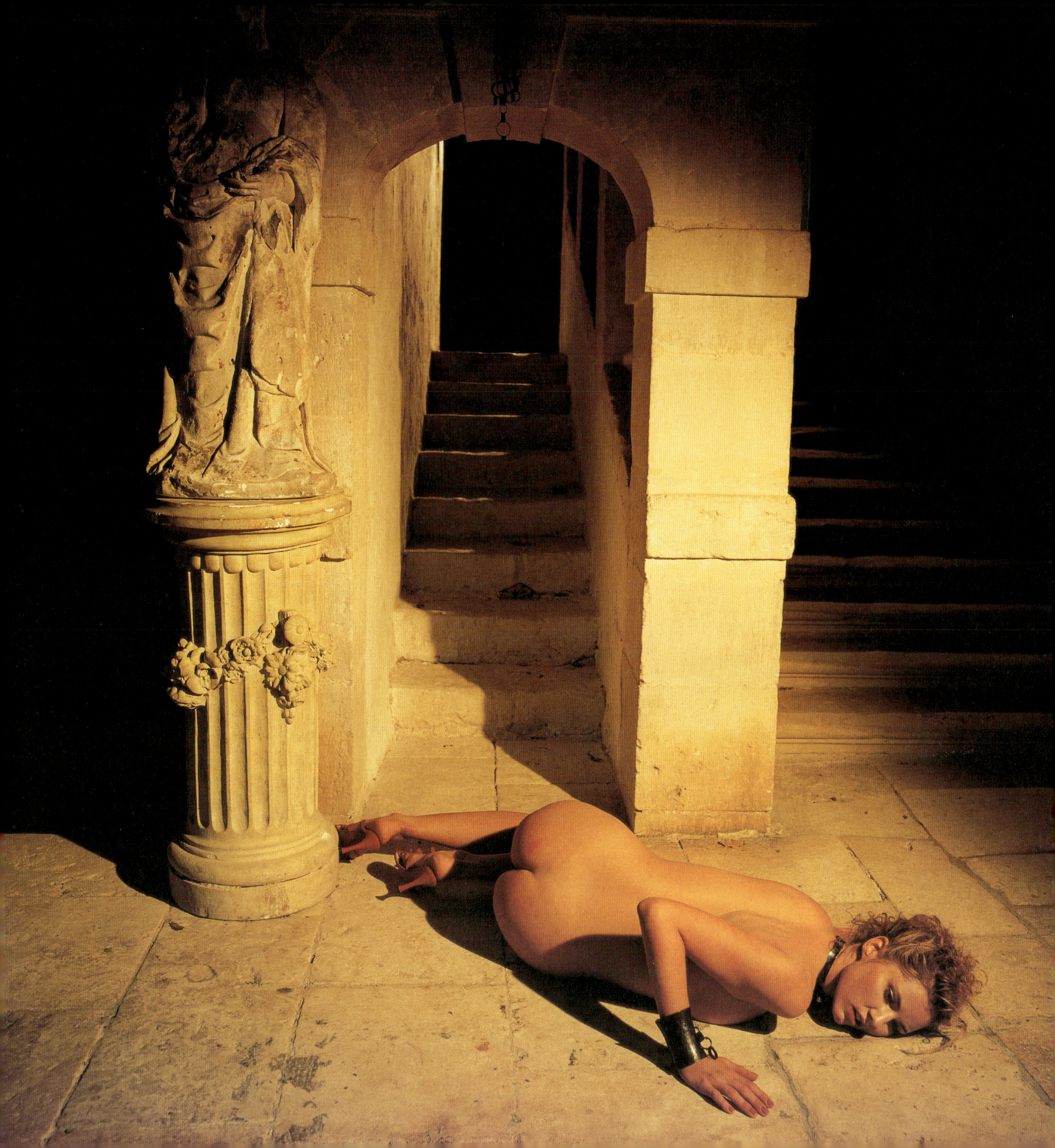

. . . "Hurry up and eat," said Andrée. "It's nine o'clock. Afterward you can sleep till noon, and when you hear the bell it will be time to get ready for lunch. You'll bathe and fix your hair. I'll come to make you up and lace up your bodice."

"You won't be on duty till afternoon," Jeanne said. "In the library: you'll serve the coffee and liqueur and tend the fire."

"And what about you?" O said.

"We're only supposed to take care of you during the first twenty-four hours of your stay. After that you're on your own, and will have dealings only with the men. We won't be able to talk to you, and you won't be able to talk to us either."

"Don't go," O said. "Stay a while longer and tell me. . ."

But she did not have time to finish her sentence. The door opened: it was her lover, and he was not alone. . . .

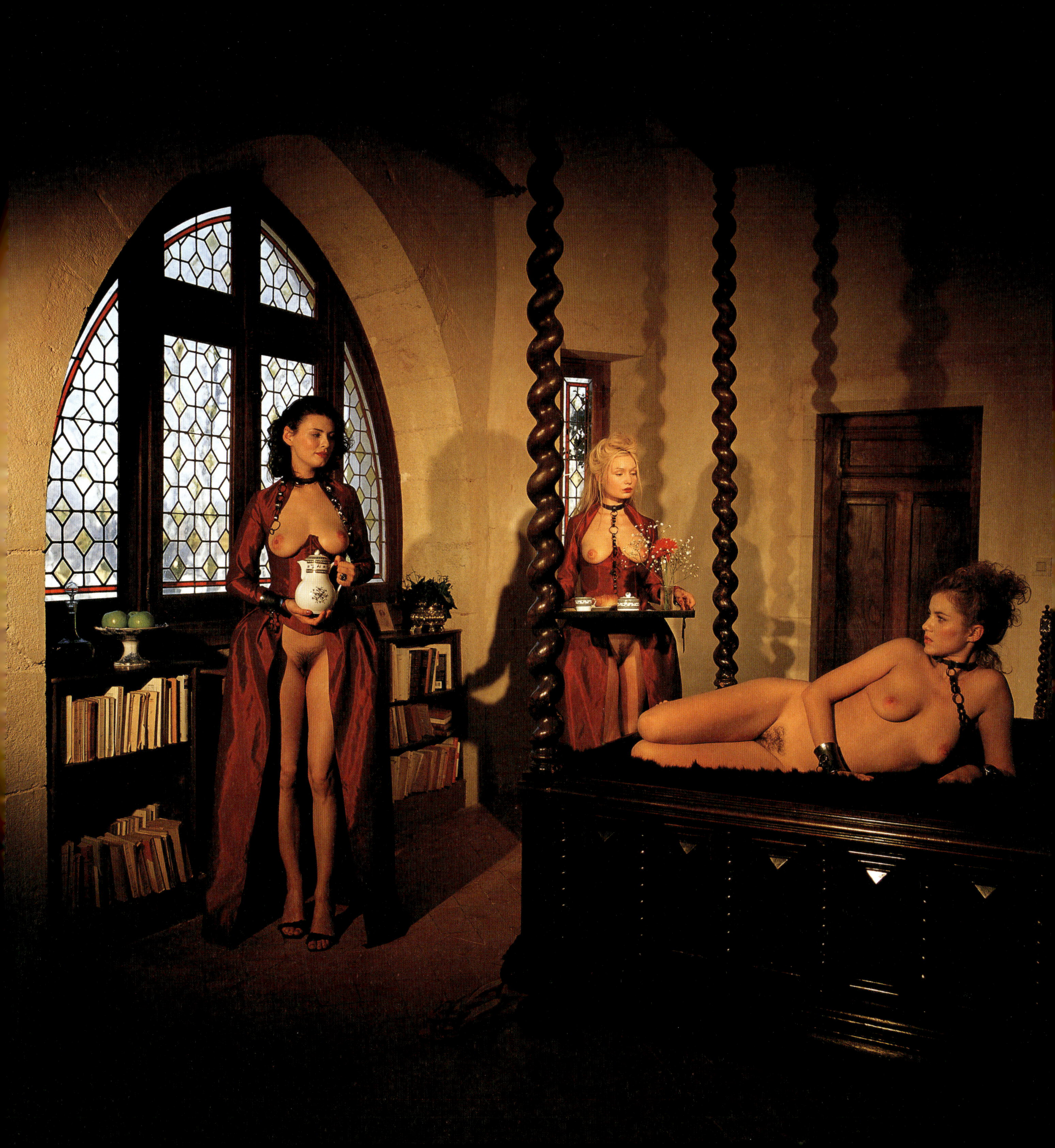

... The unknown man, whom she still did not dare to look at, then asked her, after having run his hand over her breasts and down her buttocks, to spread her legs.

"Do as he says," said René, who was holding her up. He too was standing, and her back was against him. With his right hand he was caressing one breast, and his other was on her shoulder. The unknown man had sat down on the edge of the bed, he had seized and slowly parted, drawing the fleece, the lips which protected the entrance itself. René pushed her forward, as soon as he realized what was wanted from her, so that she would become more accessible, and his right arm slipped around her waist, giving him a better grip. ...

. . . She moaned when the alien lips, which were pressing upon the mound of flesh whence the inner corolla emanates, suddenly inflamed her, left her to allow the hot tip of the tongue to inflame her even more; she moaned even more when the lips began again: she felt the hidden point harden and rise, that point caught in a long, sucking bite between teeth and lips, which did not let go, a long, soothing bite which made her gasp for breath. She lost her footing and found herself again lying on the bed, with René's mouth on her mouth; his two hands were pinning her shoulders to the bed, while two other hands beneath her knees were raising and opening her legs. . . .

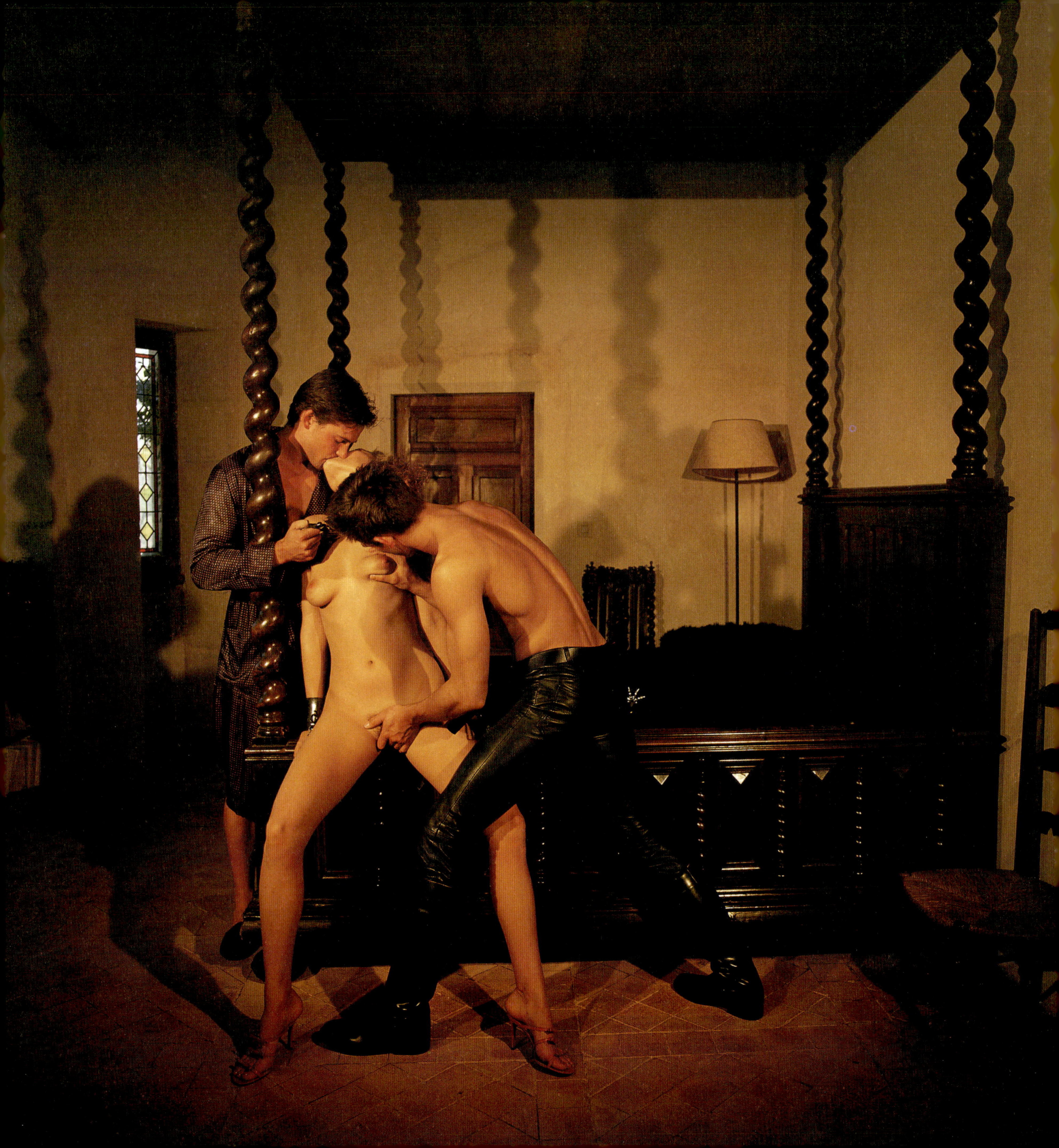

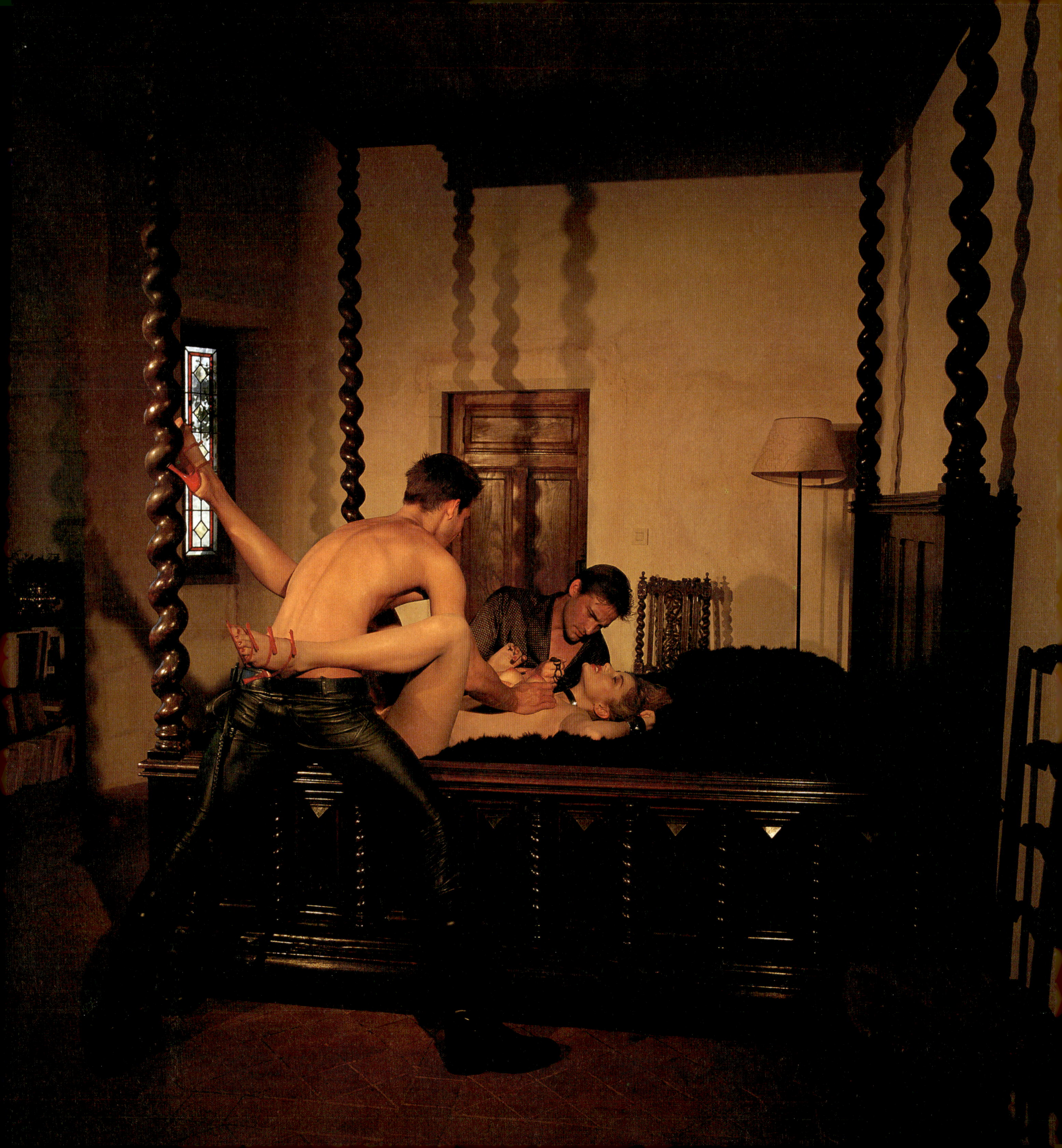

. . . Pierre fastened the chain to the ring in her collar and invited her to follow him. She got up, felt herself being pulled forward, and walked. Her bare feet were icy cold on the tiles, and she gathered she was following the hallway of the red wing; then the ground which was still as cold, became rough underfoot: she was walking on a stone floor, made of sandstone or granite. Twice the valet made her stop, she heard the sound of a key in a lock, of a lock being turned and opened, then locked again. "Careful of the steps," said Pierre, and she went down a staircase, and once she stumbled. Pierre caught her around the waist. He had never touched her except to chain or beat her, but here he was now forcing her down onto the cold steps, which she tried to grasp with her bound hands to keep from slipping, and he was taking her breasts. His mouth moved from one to the other, and as he pressed against her, she could feel him slowly rising. He did not help her up until he had taken his pleasure with her. . . .

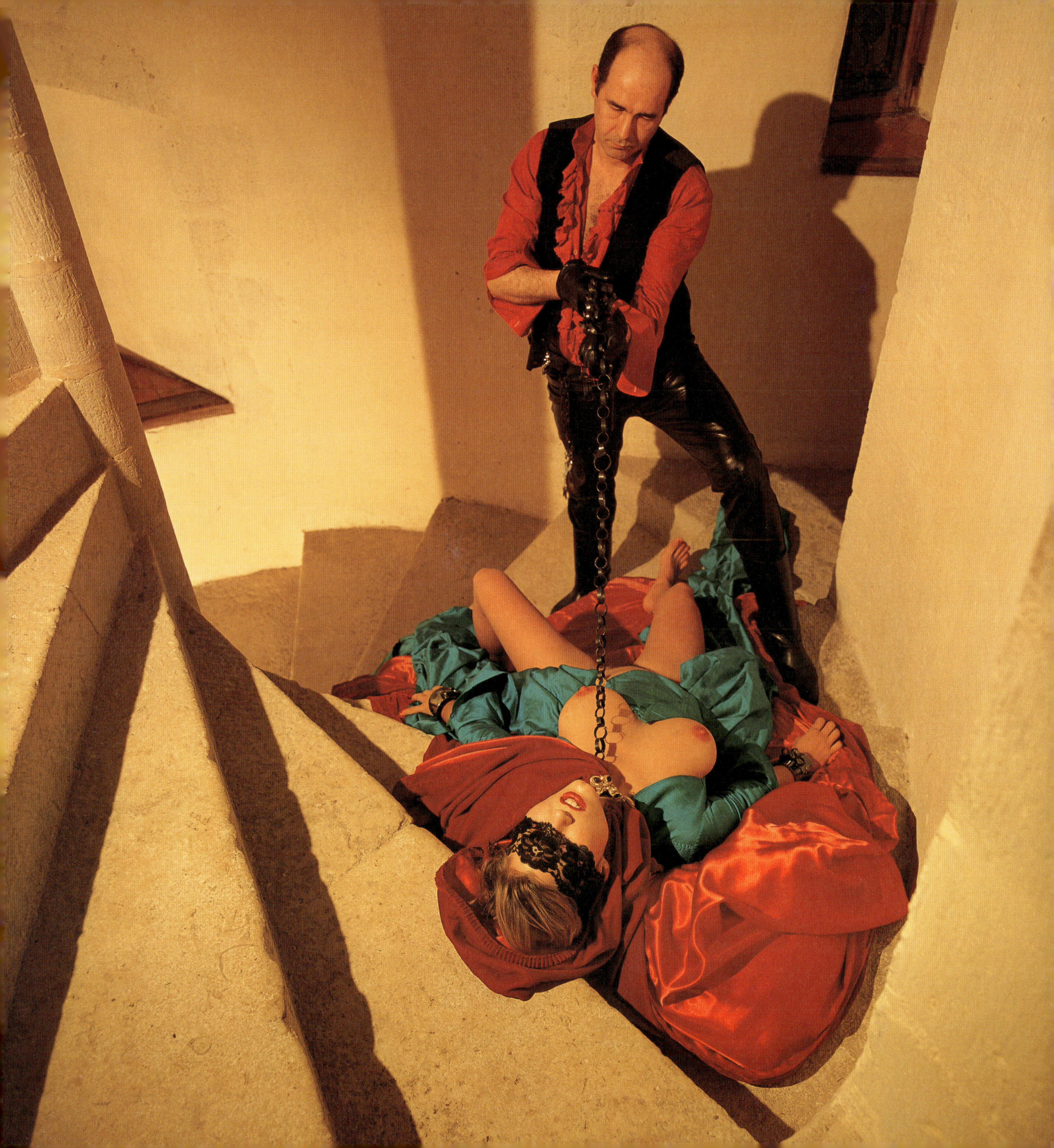

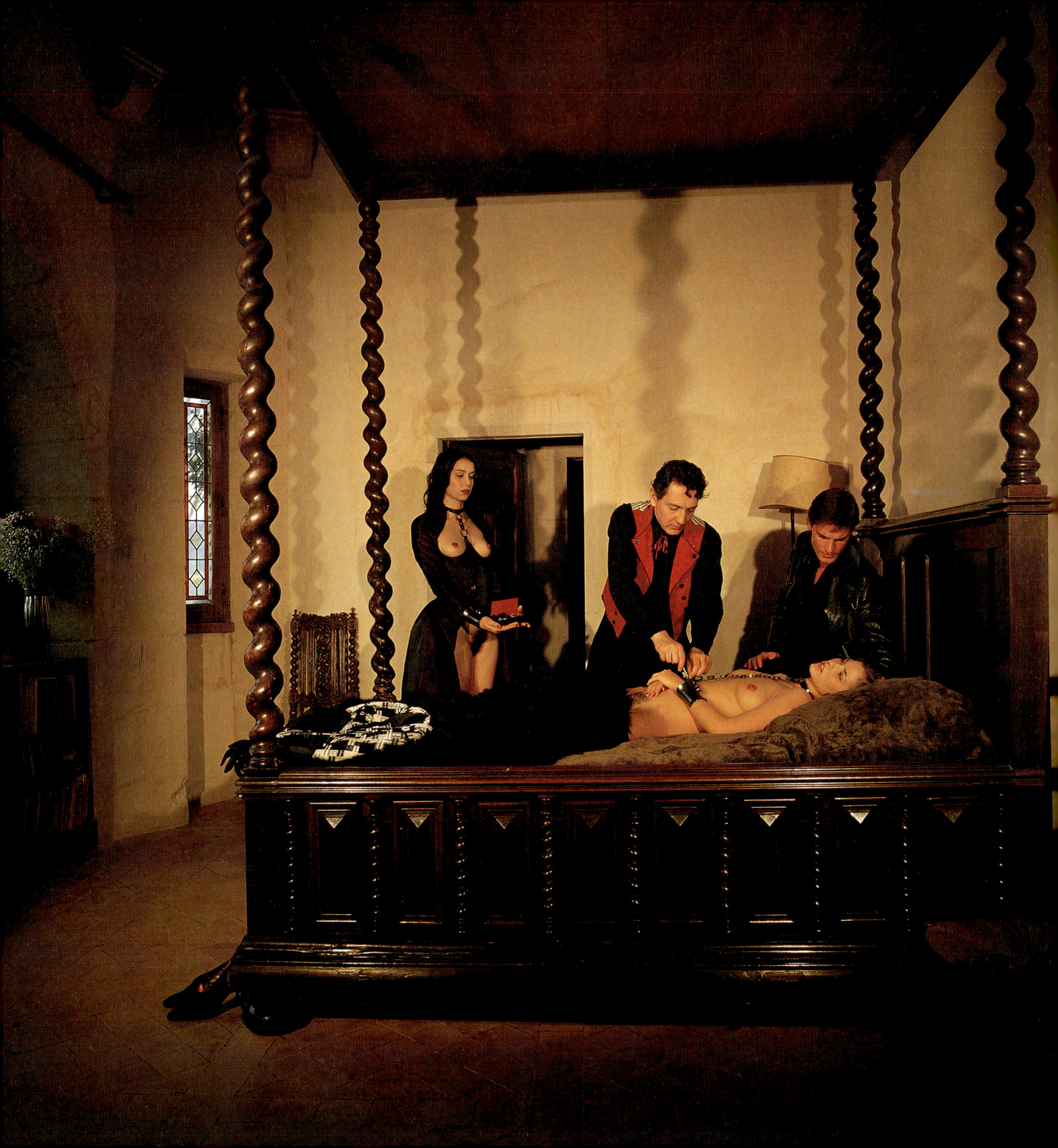

. . . the man who had explained on the first evening what would be expected of her, came in. He unlocked the collar and bracelets which had held her captive for two weeks. Was she freed of them? Or did she have the feeling something was missing? She said nothing, scarcely daring to run her hands over her wrists, not daring to lift them to her throat.

Then he asked her to choose, from among the exactly identical rings which he showed to her in a small wooden box, the one which fit her left ring finger. They were strange iron rings, banded with gold inside, and the signet was wide and as massive as that of an actual signet ring, but it was convex, and for design bore a three-spoked wheel inlaid in gold, with each spoke spiralling back upon itself like the solar wheel of the Celts. The second ring she tried, though a trifle snug, fit her exactly. It was heavy on her hand, and the gold gleamed as though furtively in the dull gray of the polished iron. . . .

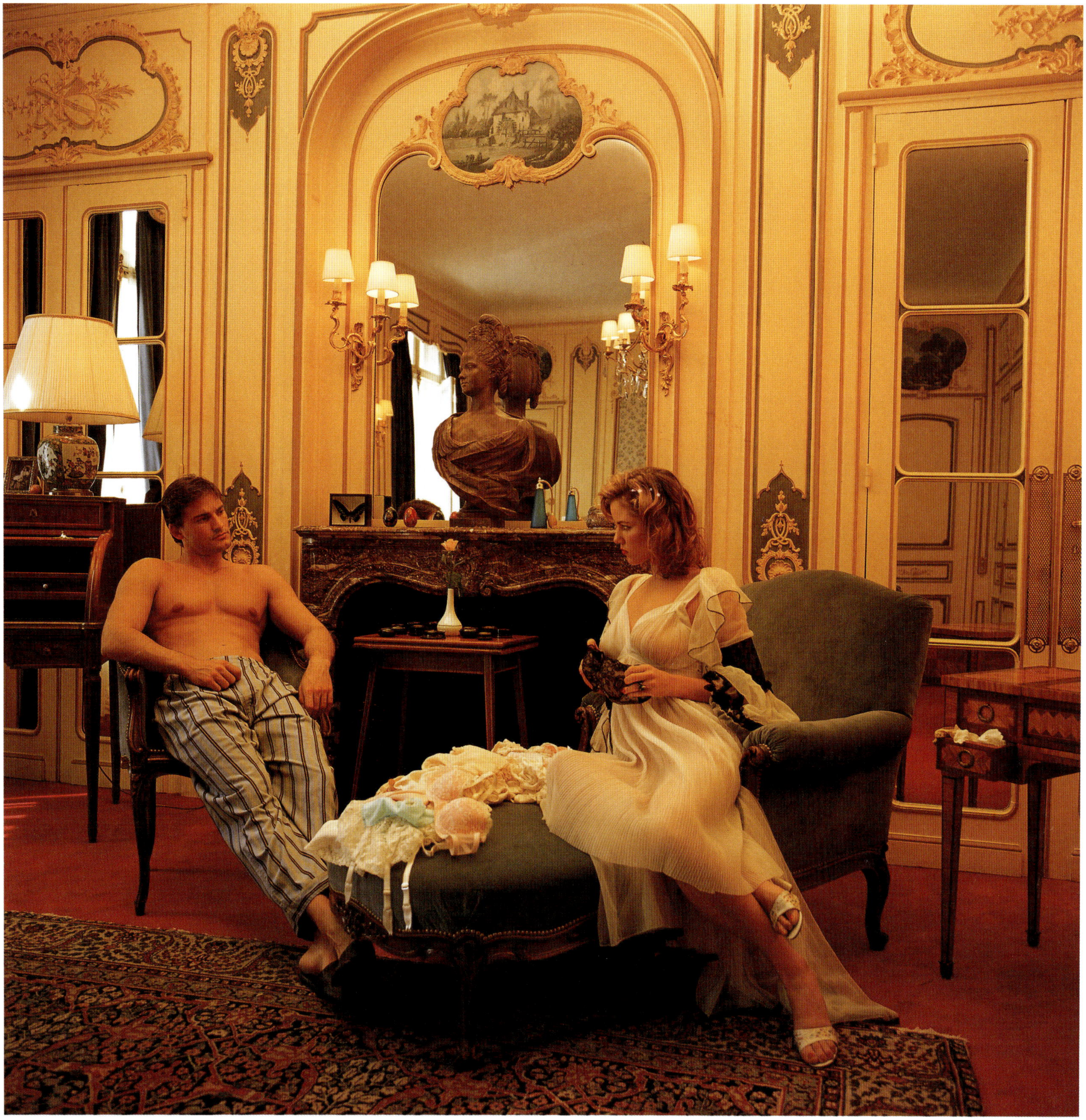

. . . O listened to her lover.

He began by saying that she should not think that she was now free. With one exception, and that was that she was free not to love him any longer, and to leave him immediately. But if she did love him, then she was in no wise free. She listened to him without saying a word, thinking how happy she was that he wanted to prove to himself—it mattered little how—that she belonged to him, and thinking too that he was more than a little naive not to realize that this proprietorship was beyond any proof. But did he perhaps realize it and want to emphasize it merely because he derived a certain pleasure from it? . . .

. . . What her lover wanted from her was very simple: that she be constantly and immediately accessible. It was not enough for him to know that she was: she was to be so without the slightest obstacle intervening, and her bearing and clothing both were to bespeak, as it were, the symbol of that availability to experienced eyes. That, he went on, meant two things. The first she knew, having been informed of it the evening of her arrival at the château: that she must never cross her knees, as her lips had always to remain open. She doubtless thought that this was nothing (that was indeed what she did think), but she would learn that to maintain this discipline would require a constant effort on her part, an effort which would remind her, in the secret they shared between them and perhaps with a few others, of the reality of her condition . . .

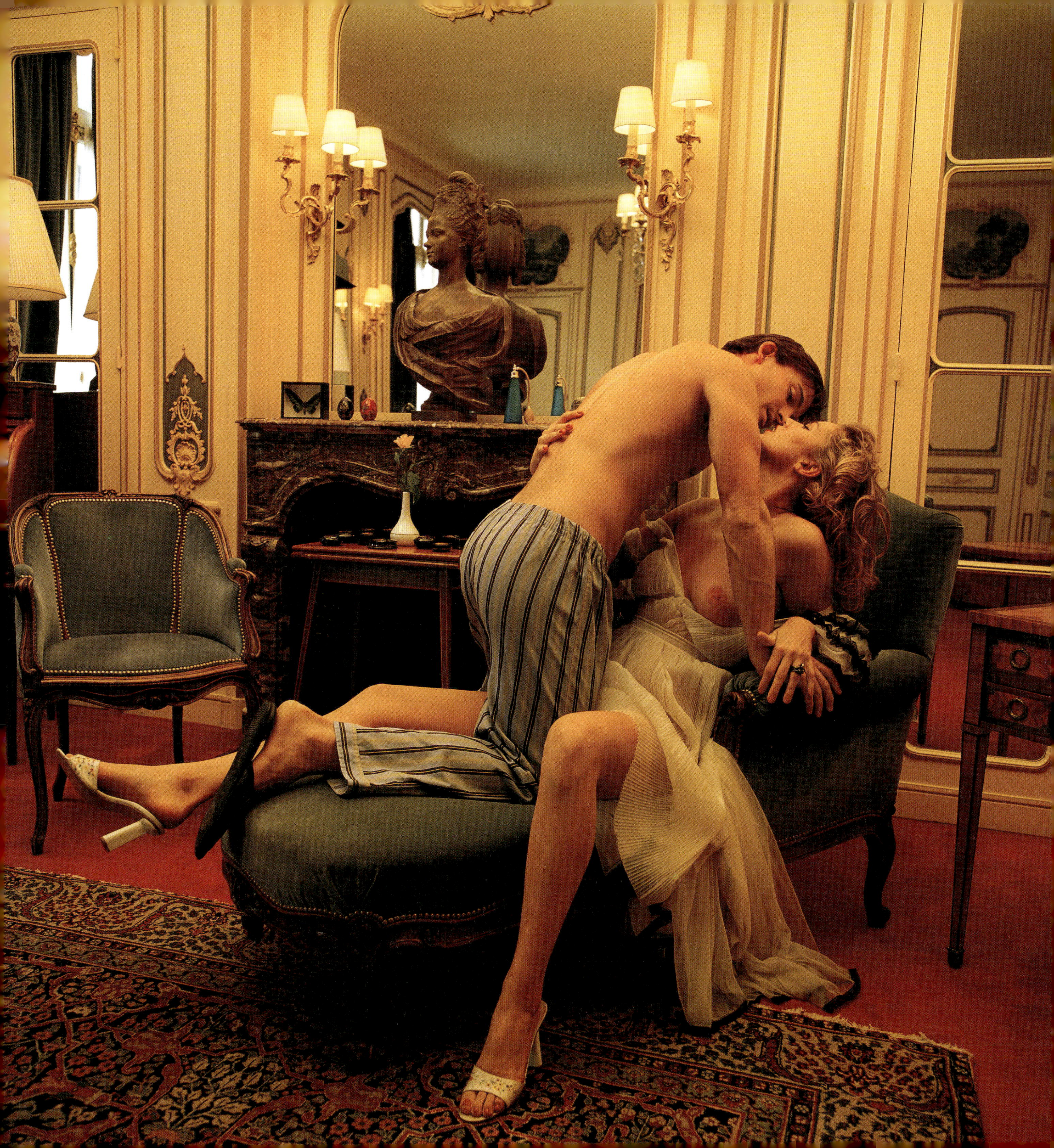

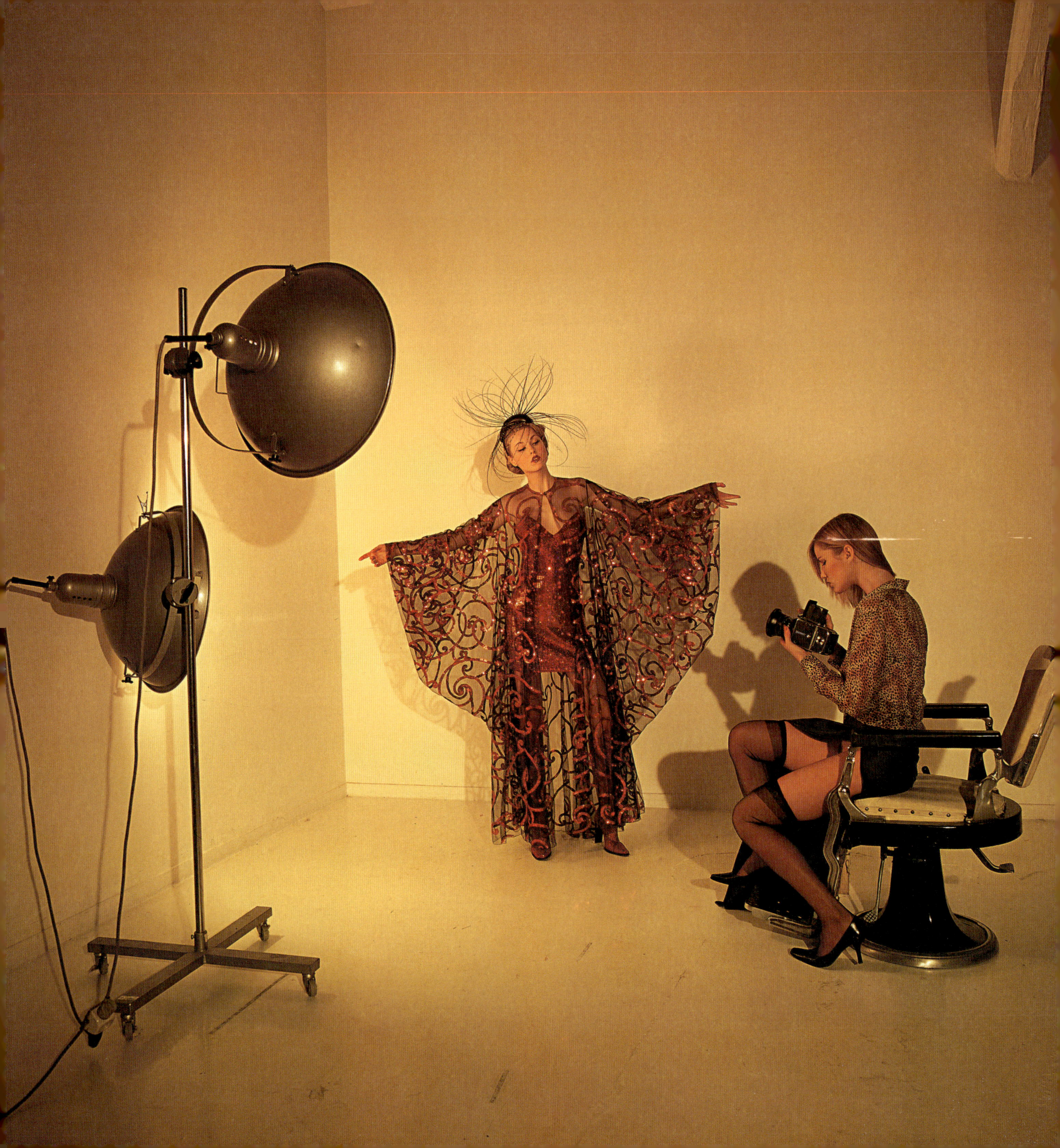

... "Very little-girl-like," one of the models said to her one day, a blond, green-eyed model with high Slavic cheekbones and the olive complexion that goes with it. "But you shouldn't wear garters," she added. "You're going to ruin your legs."

This remark was occasioned by O, who, without stopping to think, had sat down somewhat hastily in her presence, and obliquely in front of her, on the arm of a big leather easy chair, and in so doing had lifted her skirt. The tall girl had glimpsed a flash of naked thigh above the rolled stocking, which covered the knee but stopped just above it.

O had seen her smile, so strangely that she wondered what the girl had been thinking at the time, or perhaps what she had understood. She adjusted her stockings, one at a time, pulling them up to tighten them, for it was not as easy to keep them tight this way as it was when the stockings ended at mid-thigh and were fastened to a garter belt, and answered Jacqueline, as though to justify herself:

"It's practical."

"Practical for what?" Jacqueline wanted to know.

"I dislike garter belts," O replied.

But Jacqueline was not listening to her and was looking at the iron ring. ...

... During the next few days, O took some fifty photographs of Jacqueline. They were like nothing she had ever taken before. Never, perhaps, had she had such a model. Anyway, never before had she been able to extract such meaning and emotion from a face or body. And yet all she was aiming for was to make the silks, the furs, and the laces more beautiful by that sudden beauty of an elfin creature surprised by her reflection in the mirror, which Jacqueline became ...

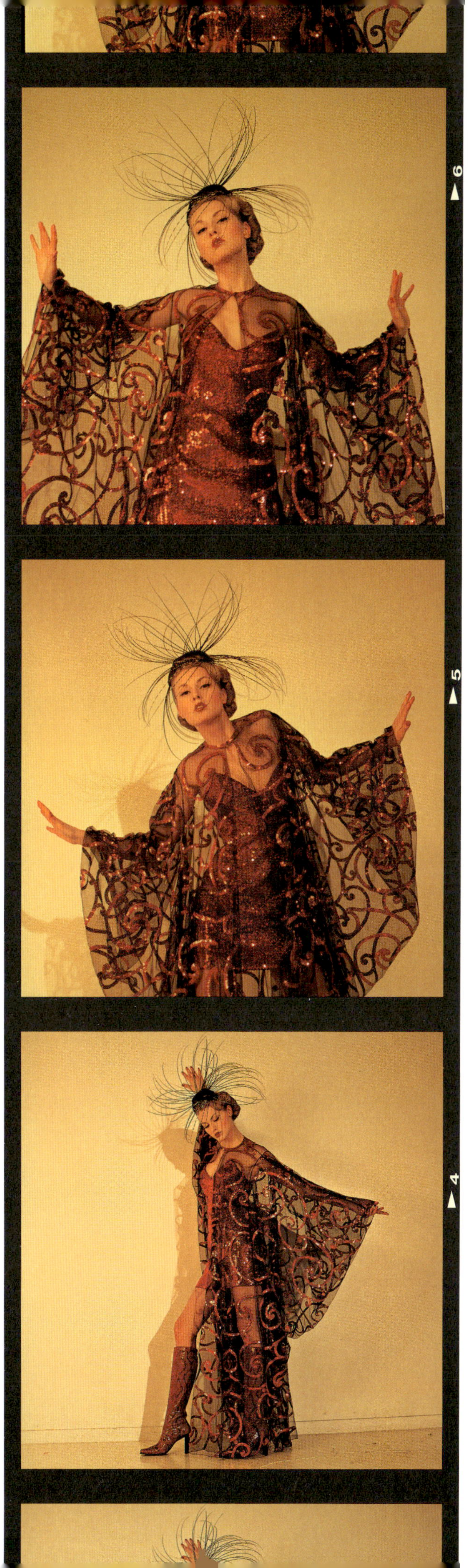

6
5
4

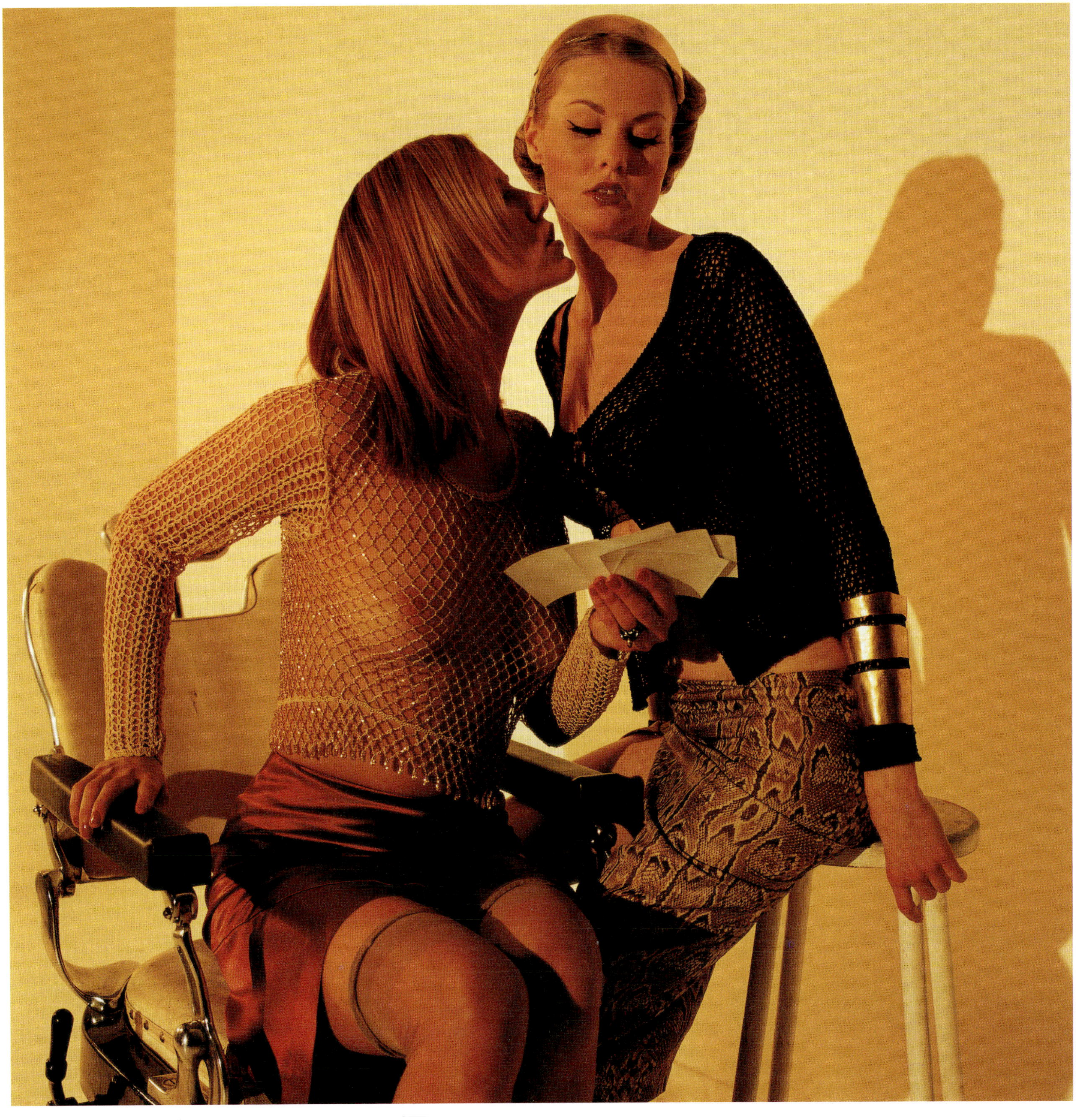

. . . And then she did something she had never done before: she followed Jacqueline into the large dressing room adjacent to the studio, where the models dressed and made up and where they left their clothing and make-up kits after hours. She remained standing, leaning against the doorjamb, her eyes glued to the mirror of the dressing table before which Jacqueline, without removing her gown, had sat down. The mirror was so big—it covered the entire back wall, and the dressing table itself was a simple slab of black glass—that she could see Jacqueline's and her own reflection, as well as the reflection of the costume girl who was undoing the aigrettes and the tulle netting. Jacqueline removed the choker herself, her bare arms lifted like two handles; a touch of perspiration gleamed in her armpits, which were shaved (Why? O wondered, what a pity, she's so fair), and O could smell the sharp, delicate, slightly plantlike odor and wondered what perfume Jacqueline ought to wear—what perfume they would make her wear. . . .

... The Englishman, who had bowed without uttering a word, had not taken his eyes off her, she saw that he was looking at her knees, her hands, and finally at her lips—but so calmly and with such precise attention, with such self-assurance, that O felt herself being weighed and measured as the instrument she knew full well she was, and it was as though compelled by his gaze and, so to speak, in spite of herself that she withdrew her gloves: she knew that he would speak when her hands were bare— because she had unusual hands, more like those of a young boy than the hands of a woman, and because she was wearing on the third finger of her left hand the iron ring with the triple spiral of gold. But no, he said nothing, he smiled: he had seen the ring. ...

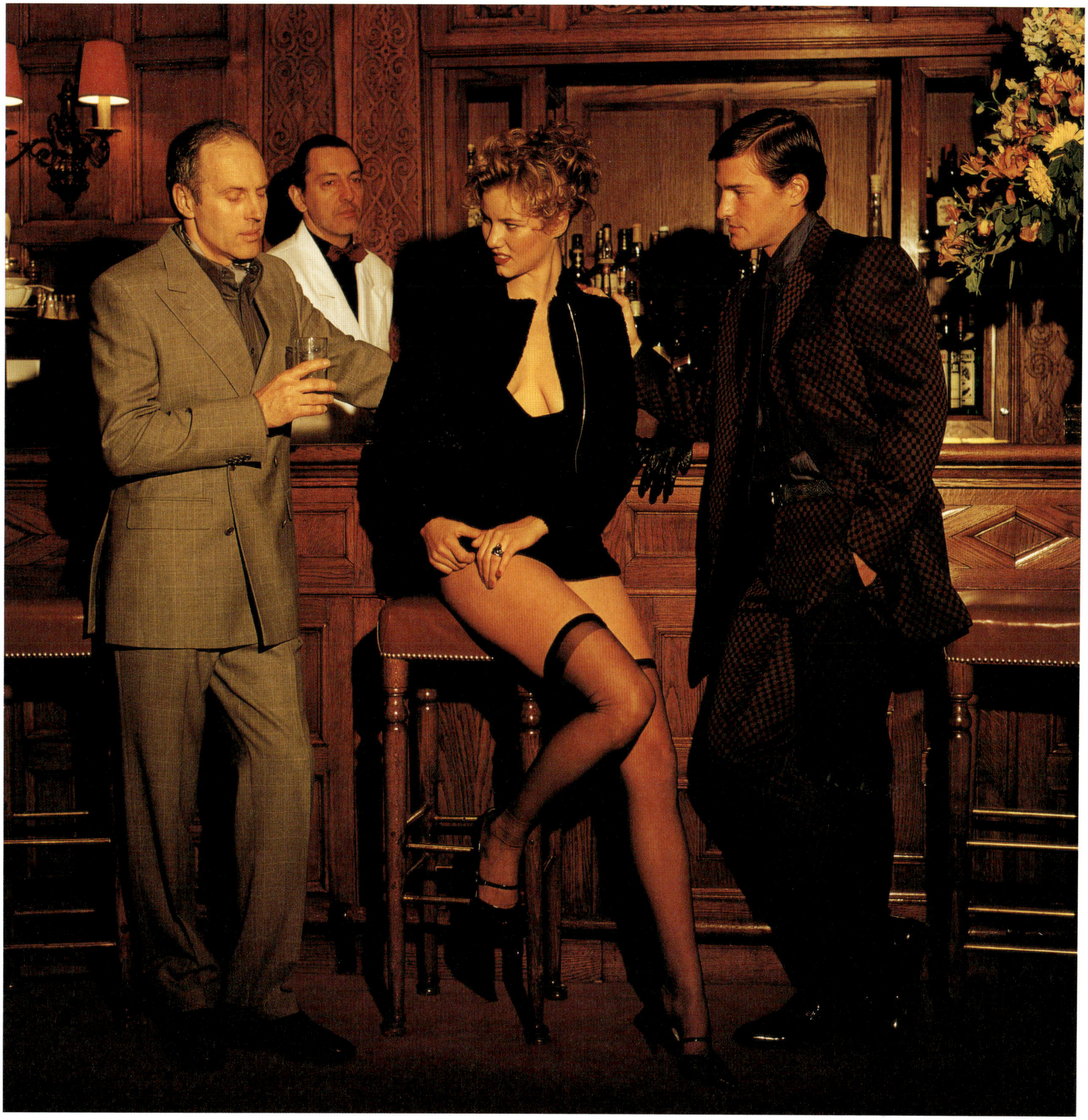

. . . O took off her fur and lay it over the back of the sofa. When she turned around, she noticed that her lover and her host were standing waiting for her to accept Sir Stephen's invitation. When, when would she ever learn, and would she ever learn, a gesture stealthy enough so that when she lifted her skirt no one would notice, so that she herself could forget her nakedness, her submission? Not, in any case, as long as René and that stranger were staring at her in silence, as they were presently doing. Finally she gave in. . . .

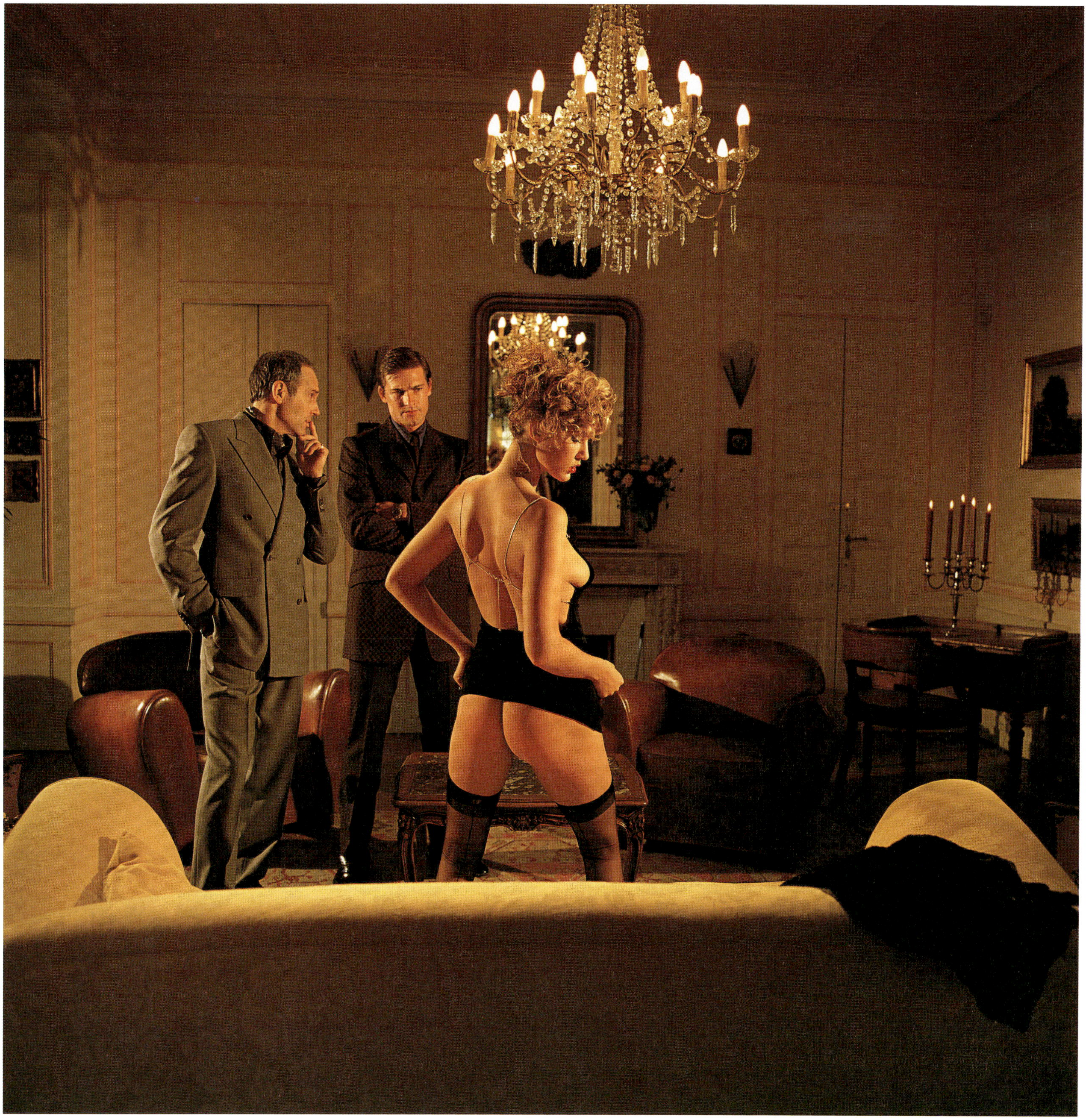

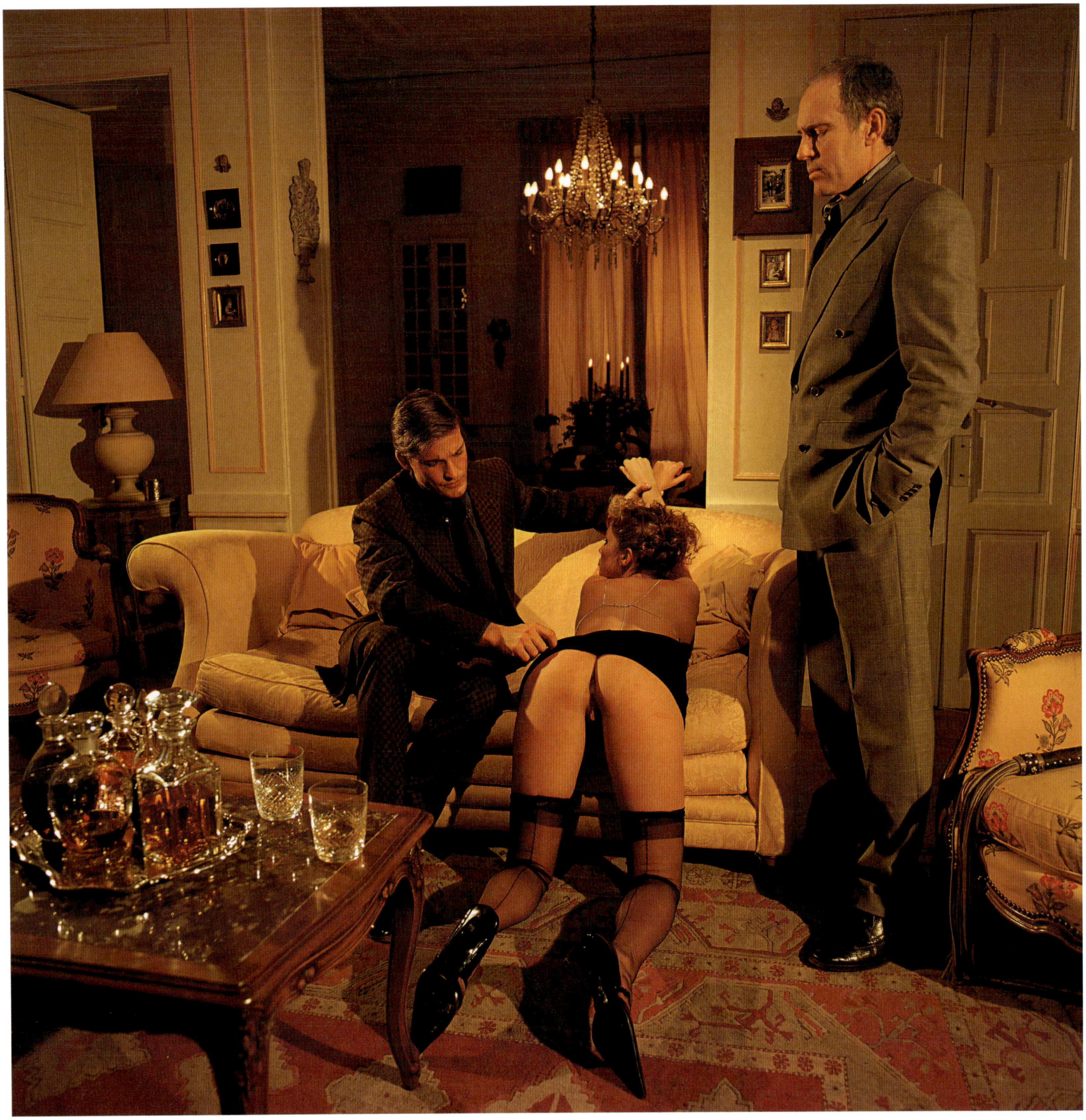

. . . With one hand, René took her wrists in a viselike grip, and with the other lifted her skirts so high that she could feel the muslin lining brush her cheek. He caressed her flanks and drew Sir Stephen's attention to the two dimples that graced them, and the softness of the furrow between her thighs. Then, with that same hand, he pressed her waist to accentuate further her buttocks, and ordered her to open her knees wider. She obeyed without saying a word . . .

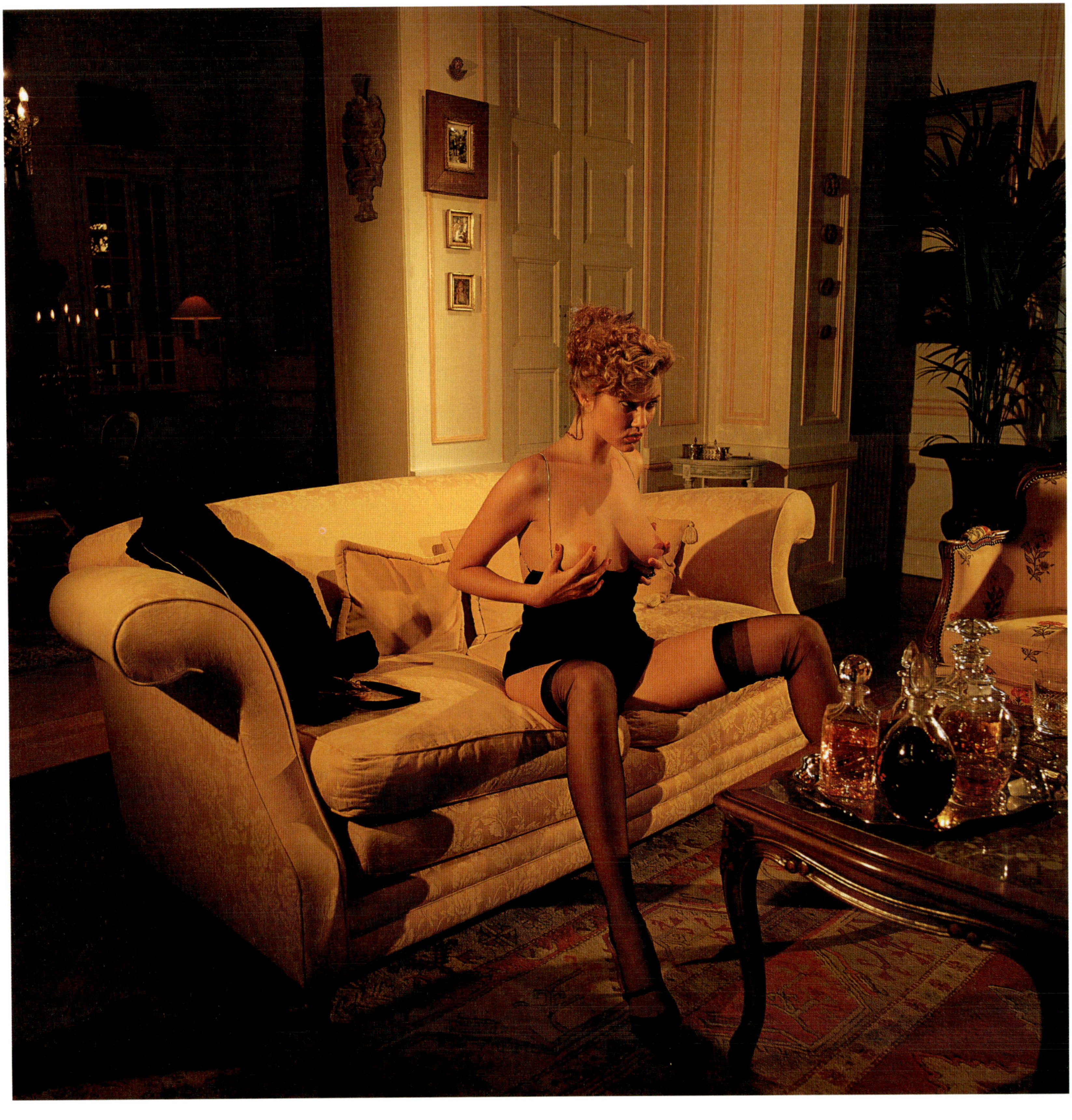

. . . O unhooked the large gold hooks and slipped her close-fitting jacket down over her shoulders; then she put it at the other end of the sofa, where her fur, her gloves, and her bag were.

"Caress the tips of your breasts, ever so lightly," Sir Stephen said then, before adding: "You must use a darker rouge, yours is too light."

Taken completely aback, O fondled her nipples with her fingertips and felt them stiffen and rise. . . .

. . . She struggled and clenched her teeth with rage when, having made her bend over, with her elbows on the floor and her head between her arms, her buttocks raised, he forced her from behind, to rend her as René had said he would.

The first time she did not cry out. He went at it again, harder now, and she screamed. She screamed as much out of revolt as of pain, and he was fully aware of it. She also knew—which meant that in any event she was vanquished—that he was pleased to make her cry out. . . .

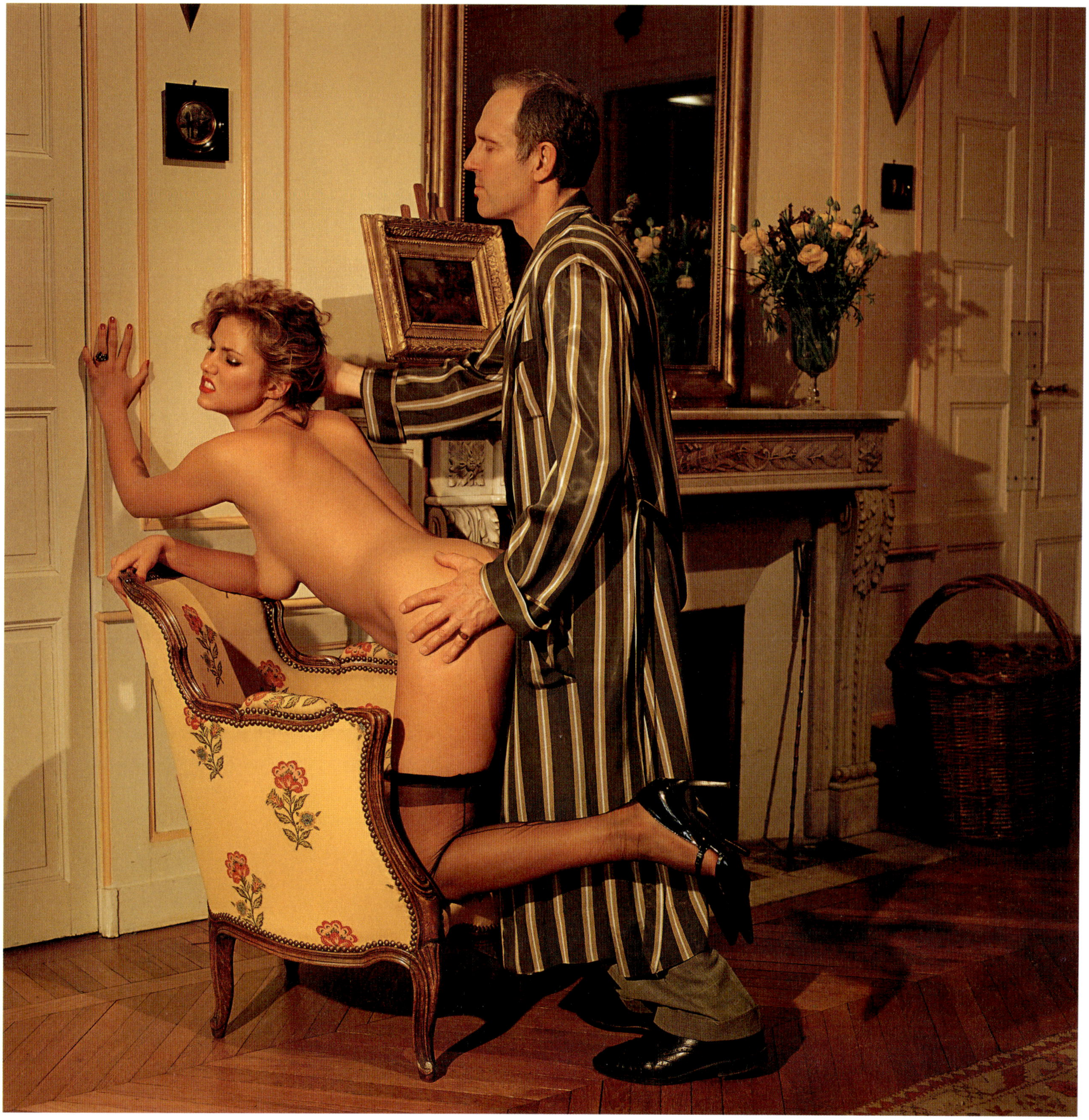

. . . she surrendered herself completely. And for the first time, so gentle were her yielding eyes when they fastened on Sir Stephen's pale, burning gaze, that he suddenly spoke to her in French, employing the familiar *tu* form with her:

"I'm going to put a gag in your mouth, O, because I'd like to whip you till I draw blood. Do I have your permission?"

"I'm yours," O said. . . .

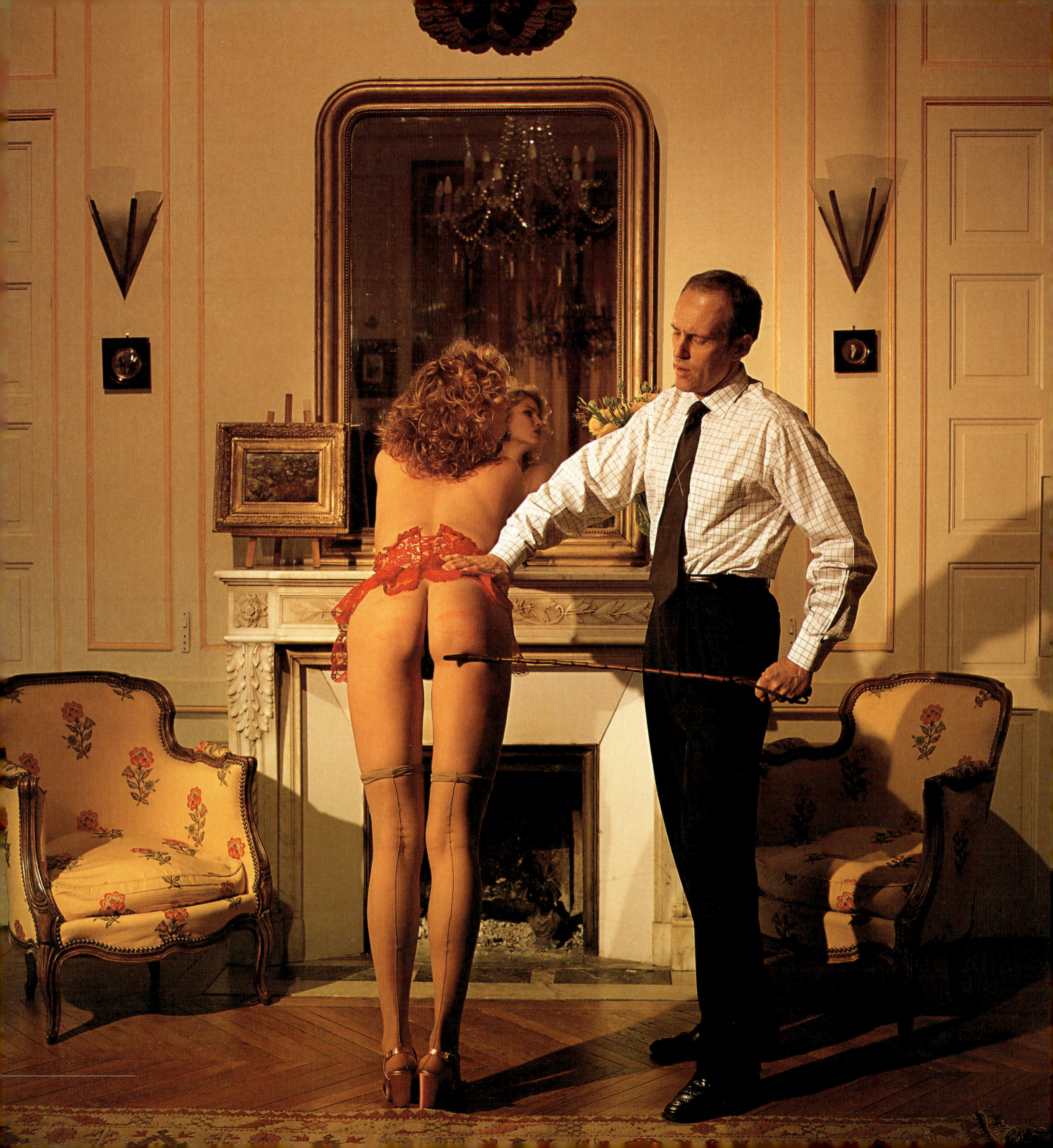

... Sir Stephen asked her whether she had any photographs of Jacqueline, and helped her to her feet so she could go and get them. It was in the living room that René, entering out of breath, for he had dashed up the four flights of stairs, came upon them: O was standing in front of the big table on which there shone, black and white, like puddles of water in the night, all of the pictures of Jacqueline. Sir Stephen, half-seated on the table, was taking them one by one as O handed them to him, and putting them back on the table ...

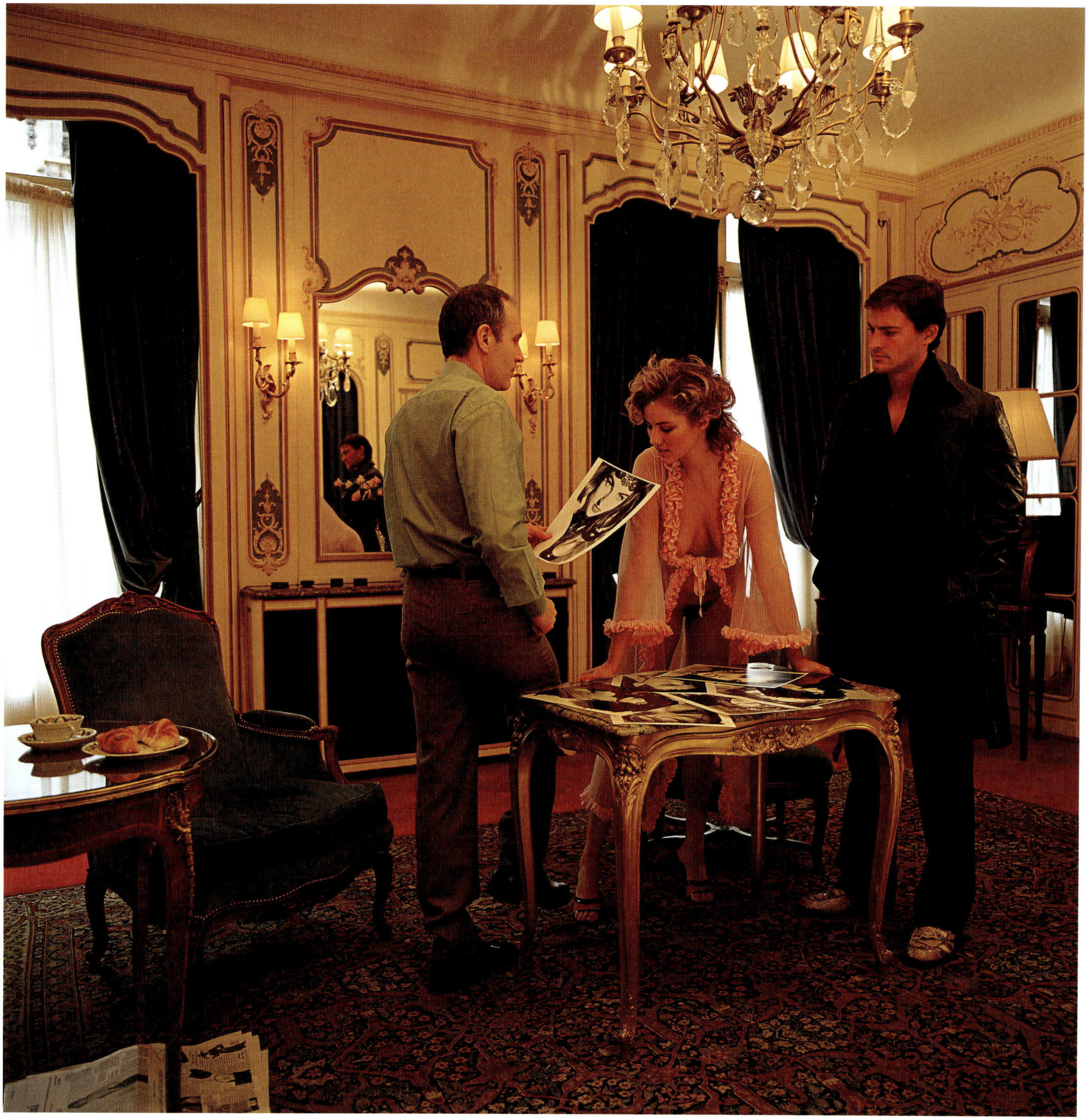

. . . The sun, falling directly on the table, curled the edges of the photographs. O wanted to move them and flatten them out to keep them from being ruined, but her fingers fumbled, she was on the verge of yielding to the probe of Sir Stephen's hand and allowing a moan to escape from her lips. She failed to hold it back, did in fact moan, and found herself sprawled flat on her back among the photographs, where Sir Stephen had rudely shoved her . . .

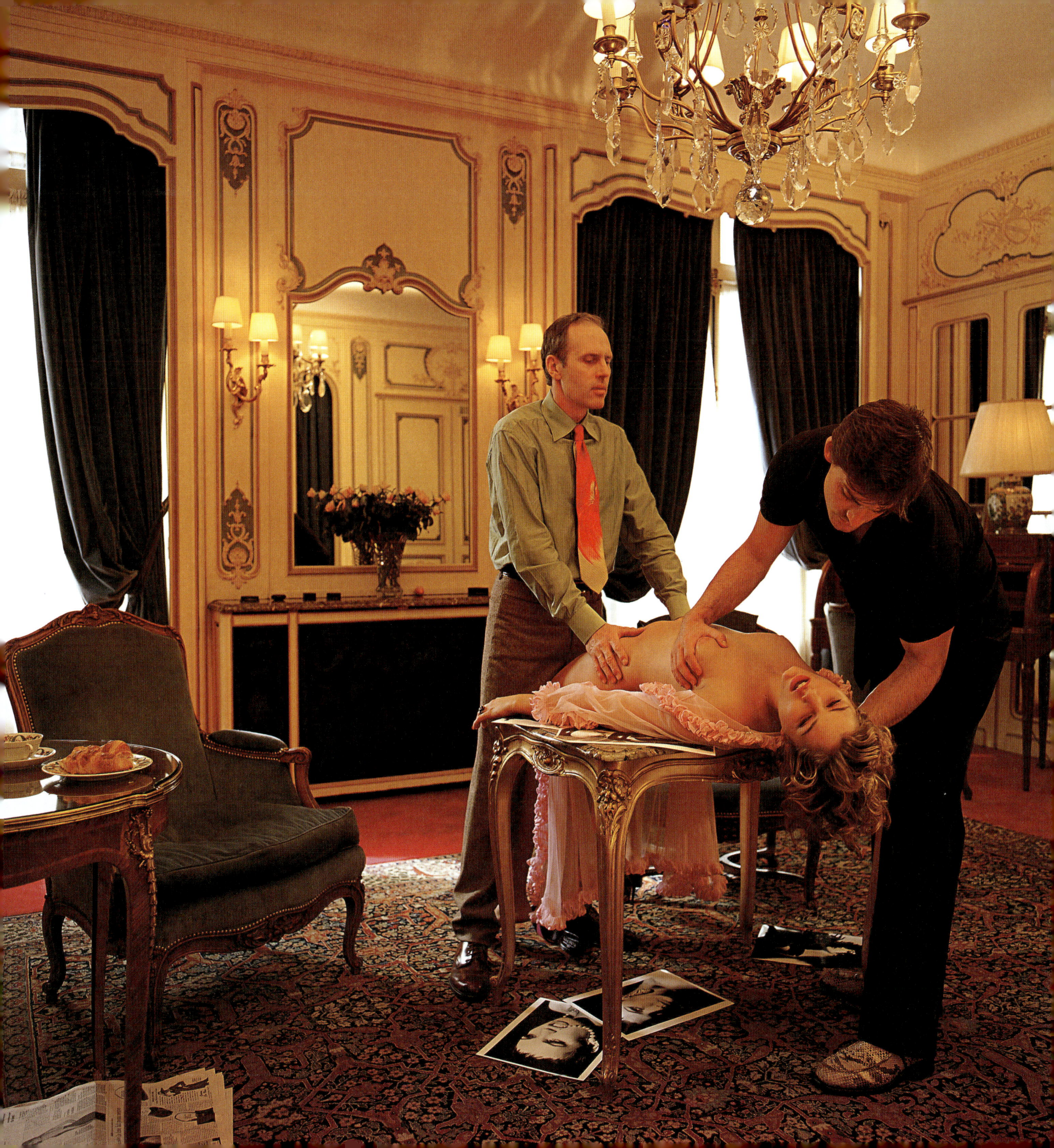

. . . Of Jacqueline it was impossible to say that she was forbearing or that she was on her guard. When she yielded to the kisses—and all she had so far granted O were kisses, which she accepted without returning—she yielded abruptly and, it seemed, totally, as though for ten seconds, or five minutes, she had become someone else. The rest of the time she was both coquettish and coy, incredibly clever at parrying an attack, contriving never to lay herself open either to a word or gesture, or even a look which would allow the victor to coincide with the vanquished or give O to believe that it was all that simple to take possession of her mouth. . . .

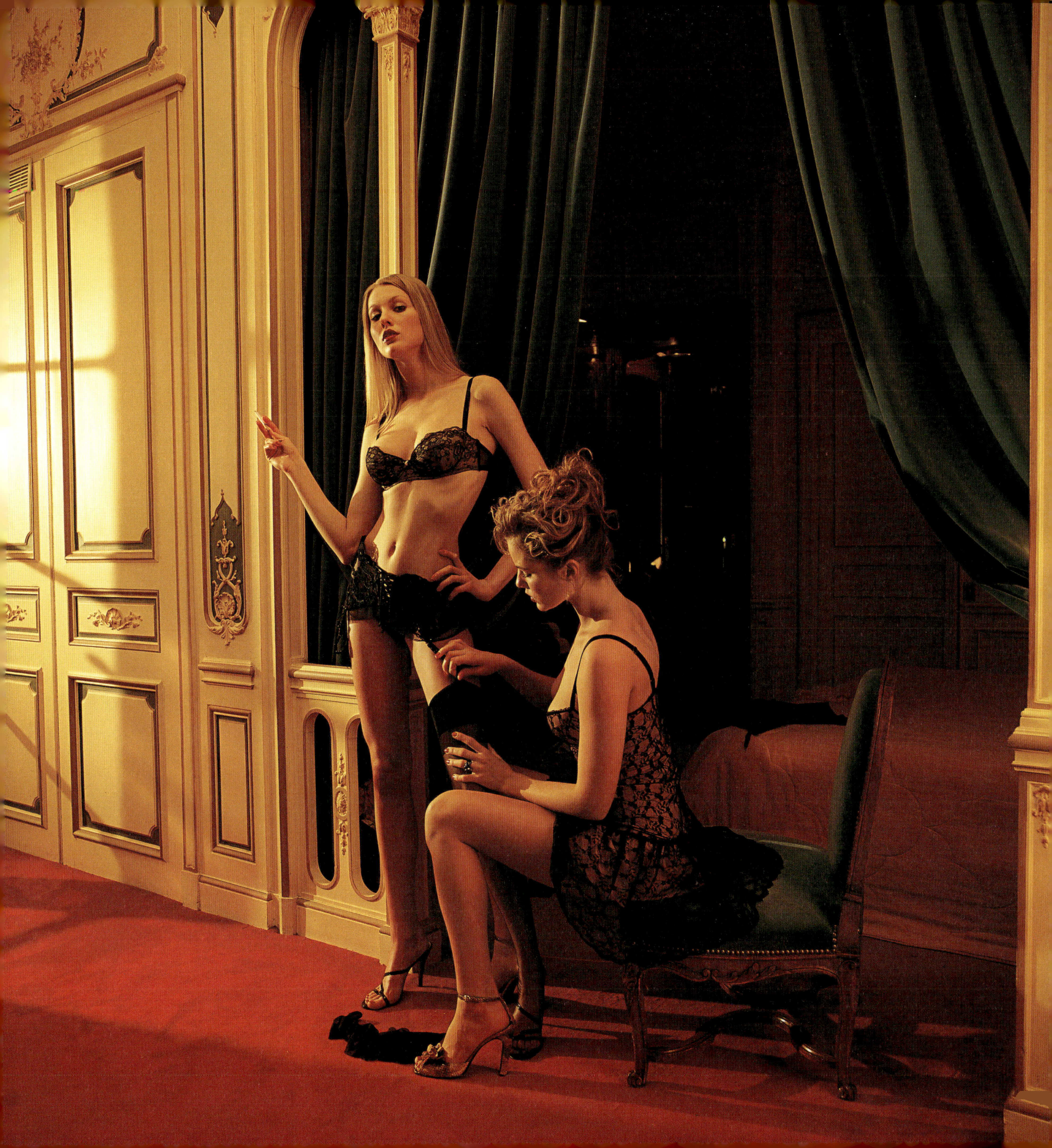

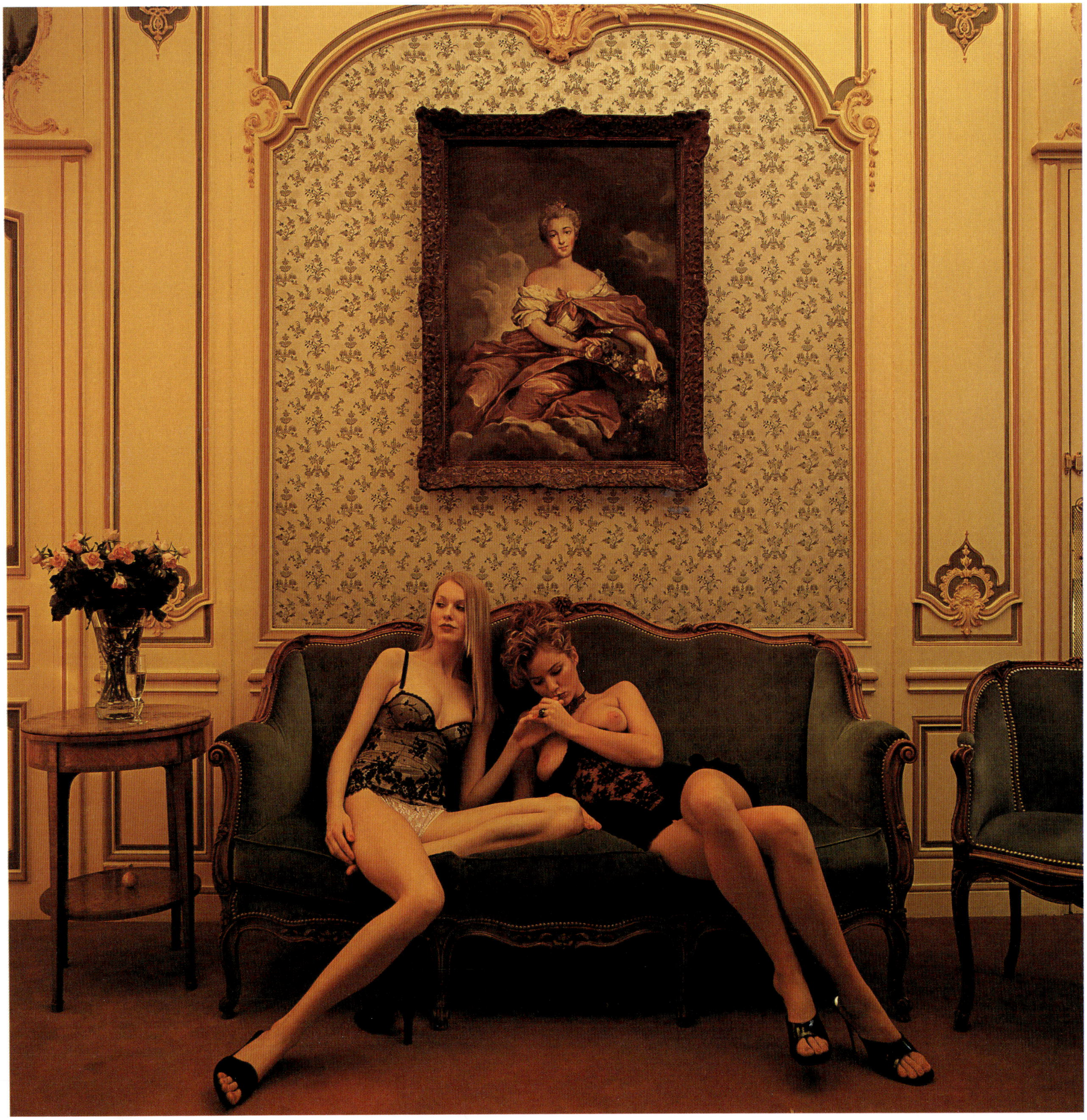

. . . In the morning she would drag herself out of bed more in anger than with any show of enthusiasm, would take her shower, quickly make herself up, for breakfast would accept only the large cup of black coffee that O barely had time to make for her, and would let O kiss the tips of her fingers, responding with no more than a mechanical smile and an expression full of malice . . .

. . . Anne-Marie lived not far from the Observatoire in Paris, in an apartment flanked by a large kind of studio, on the top floor of a new building overlooking the treetops. She was a slender woman, the same age more or less as Sir Stephen, and her black hair was streaked with gray. Her eyes were such a deep blue they looked black. She offered O and Sir Stephen some coffee, a very strong bitter coffee which she served steaming hot in tiny cups, and which reassured O. When she had finished her coffee and got up from her chair to put her empty cup on a coffee table, Anne-Marie seized her by the wrist and, turning to Sir Stephen, said:

"May I?" . . .

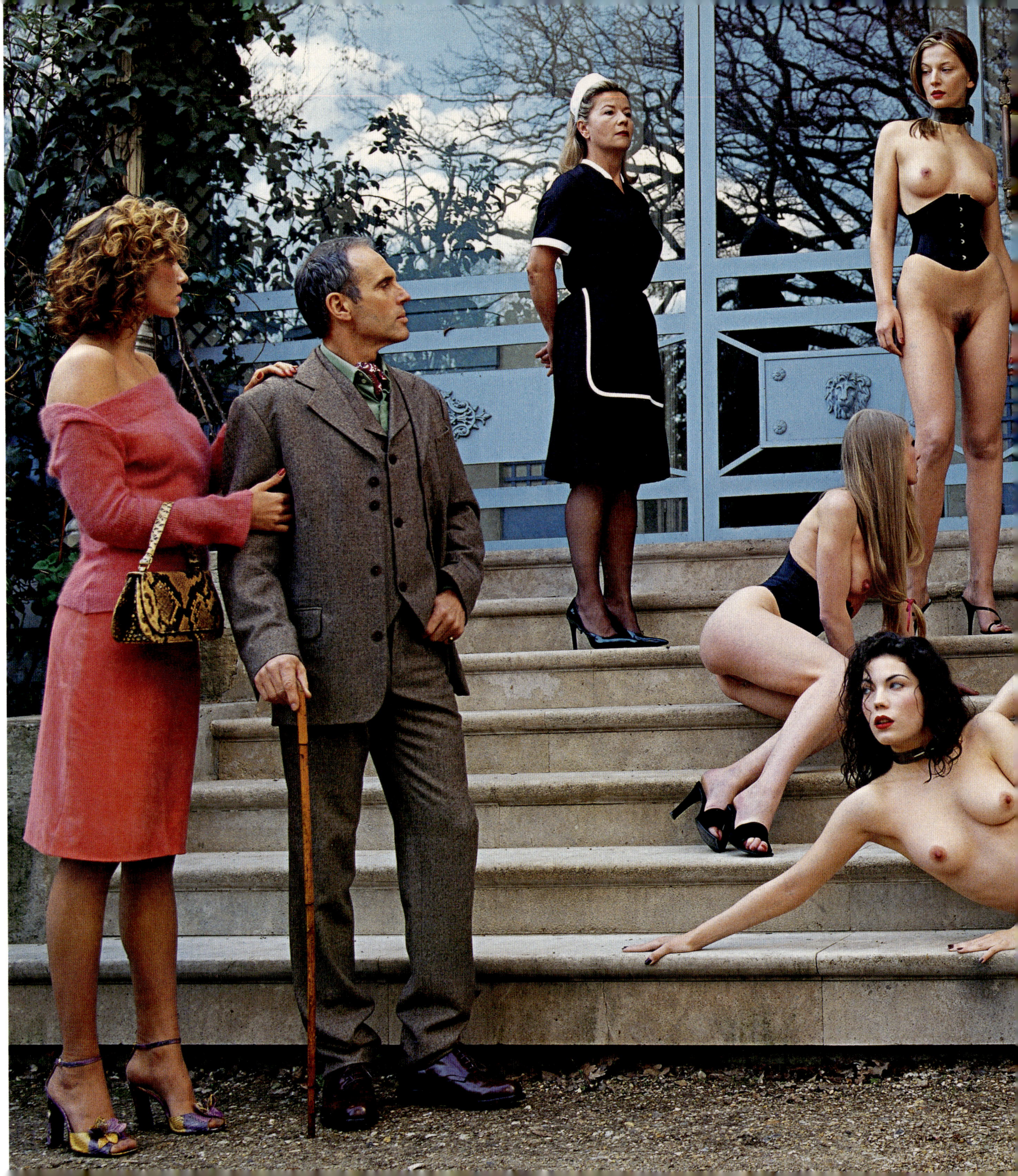

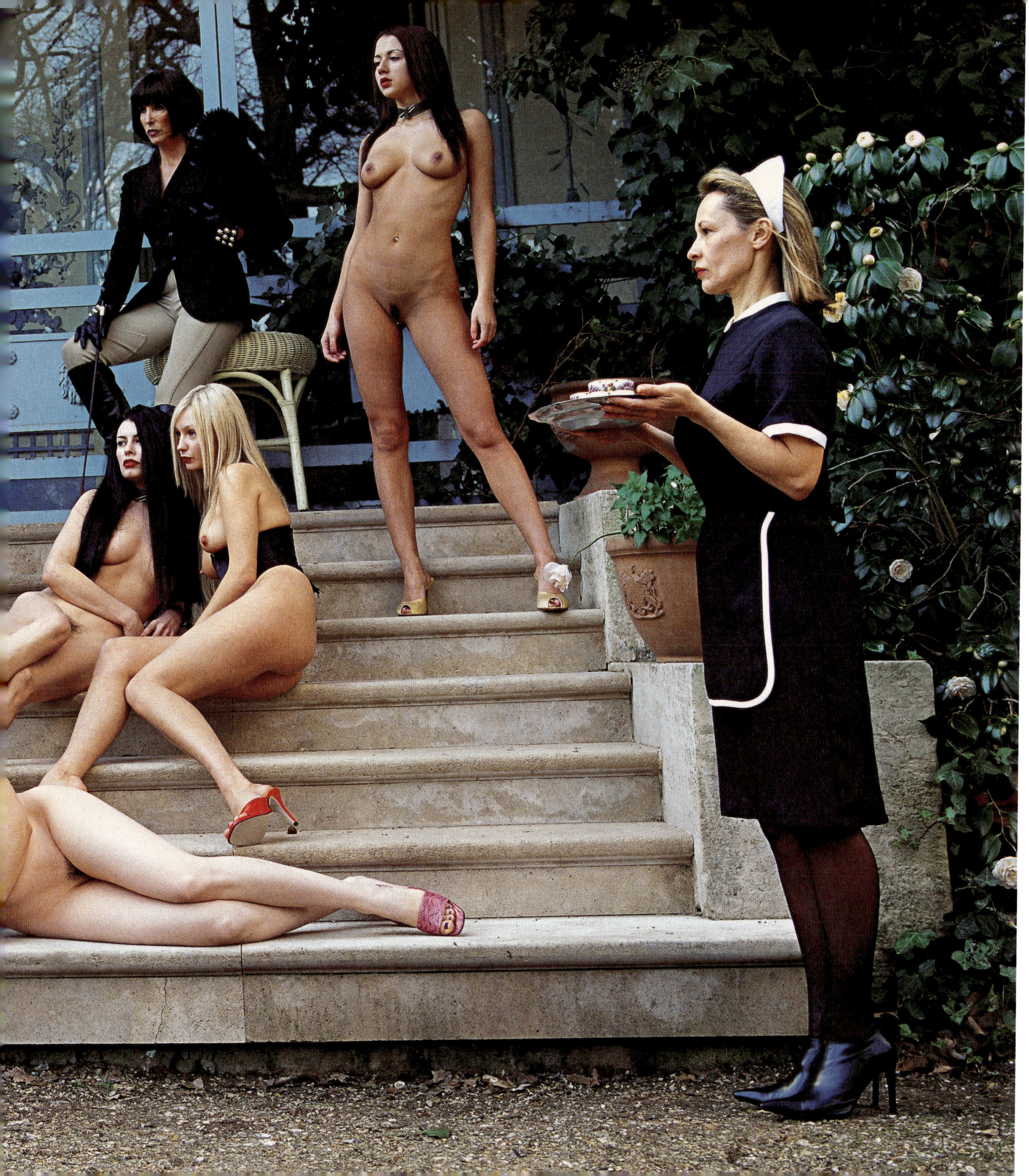

... " I'm going to give you some long, dark stockings, O, and a corset to hold them up. But it will be a whalebone corset, one that will be snug at the waist."

When Anne-Marie had rung a young blond, silent girl had brought in some very sheer, black stockings and a tight-fitting corset of black nylon taffeta, reinforced and sustained by wide, close-set stays which curved in at the lower belly and above the hips. O, who was still standing, shifting her weight from one foot to the other, slipped on the stockings, which came to the top of her thighs. The young blonde helped her into the corset, which had a row of buckles along one of the busks on one side near the back. ...

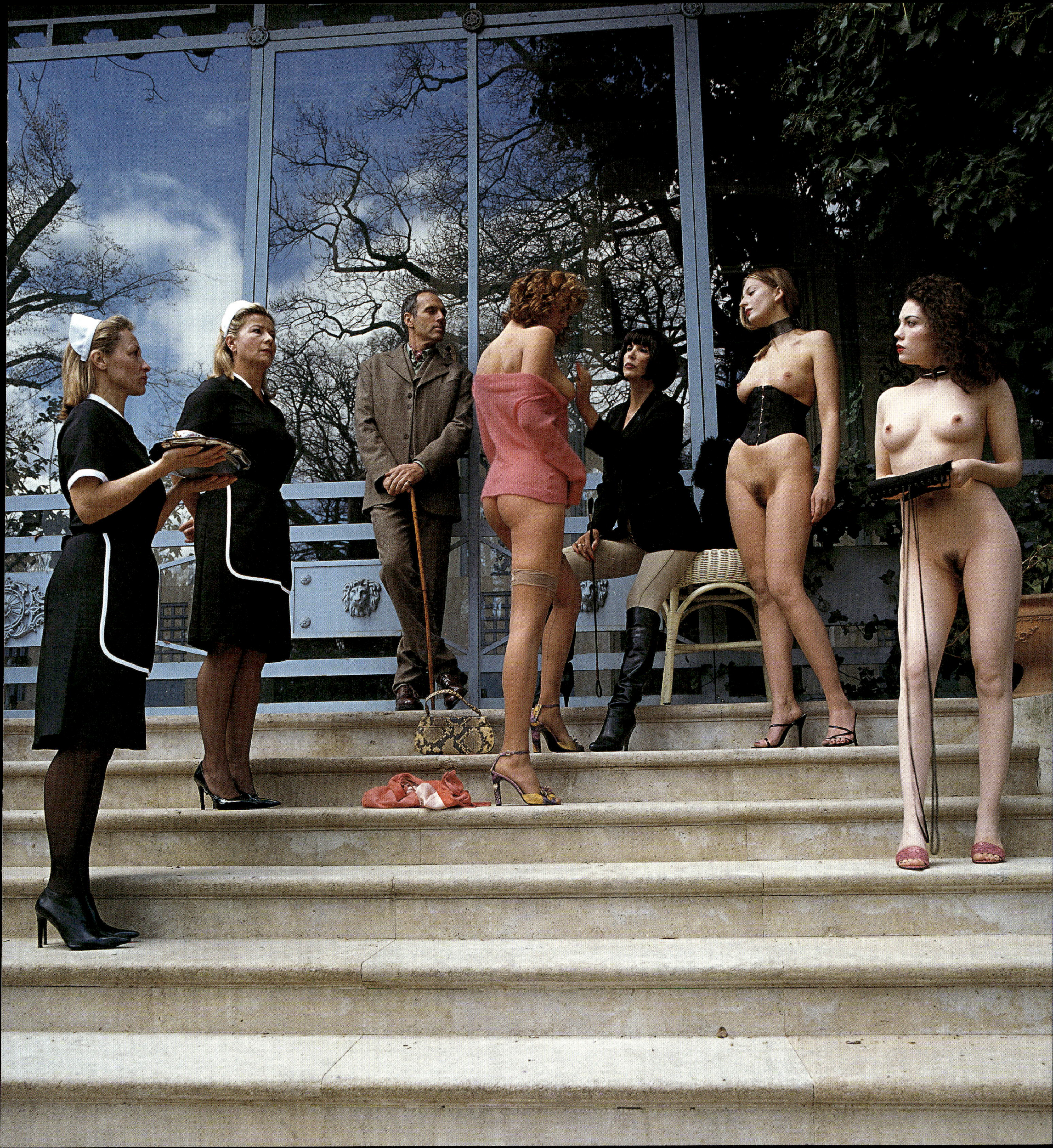

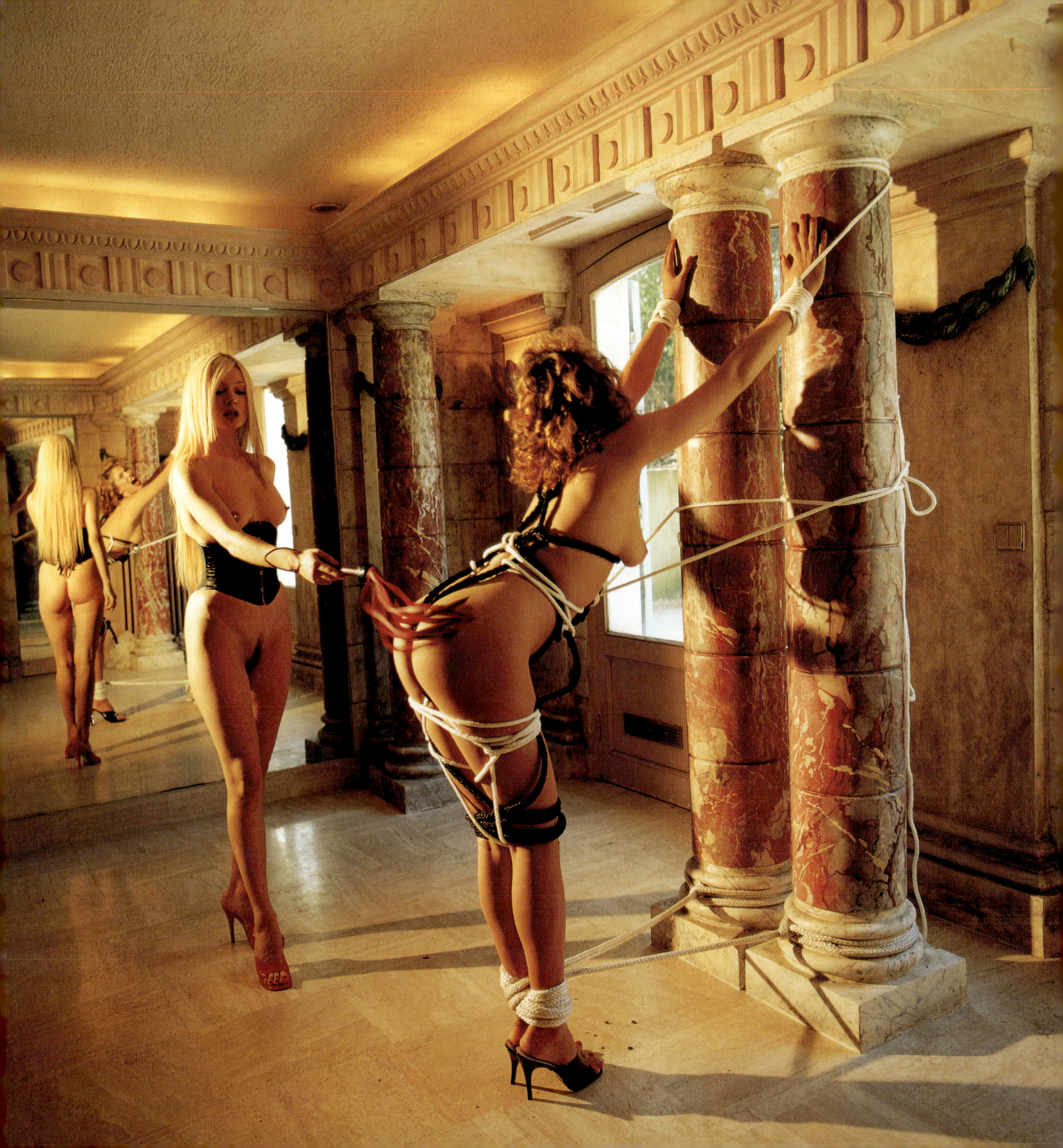

. . . As the first blows burned into her loins, O moaned. Colette alternated from left to right, paused, then started again. O struggled with all her might, she thought the straps would tear her limb from limb. She did not want to grovel, she did not want to beg for mercy. And yet that was precisely what Anne-Marie intended wringing from her lips.

"Faster," she said to Colette, "and harder."

O braced herself, but it was no use. A minute later she could bear it no more, she screamed and burst into tears, while Anne-Marie caressed her face.

"Just a second longer," she said, "and it will be over. Only five more minutes. She can scream for five minutes. It's twenty-five past, Colette. Stop when it's half past, when I tell you to."

But O was screaming:

"No, no, for God's sake don't!" screaming that she couldn't bear it, no, she couldn't bear the torture another second. And yet she endured it to the bitter end . . .

. . . "In a moment I'll pierce you, O," Anne-Marie said. "It's nothing really. What takes the longest is placing the clamps so as to be able to suture the outer and inner layers, attach the epidermis to the inner membrane. It's much easier to bear than the whip."

"You mean to say you won't put me to sleep?" O cried, trembling.

"Of course not," Anne-Marie replied. "You'll merely be tied a little more tightly than you were yesterday. That's really quite sufficient. Now come along."

A week later Anne-Marie removed the clamps and slipped on the test ring. It was lighter than it looked, for it was hollow, but still O could feel its weight. The hard metal, which was visibly piercing the flesh, looked like an instrument of torture. What would it be like when the weight of the second ring was added to it? This barbaric instrument would be immediately and glaringly apparent to the most casual glance.

"Of course it will," Anne-Marie said when O pointed this out to her. "But aren't you by now fully aware of what Sir Stephen wants? . . ."

103

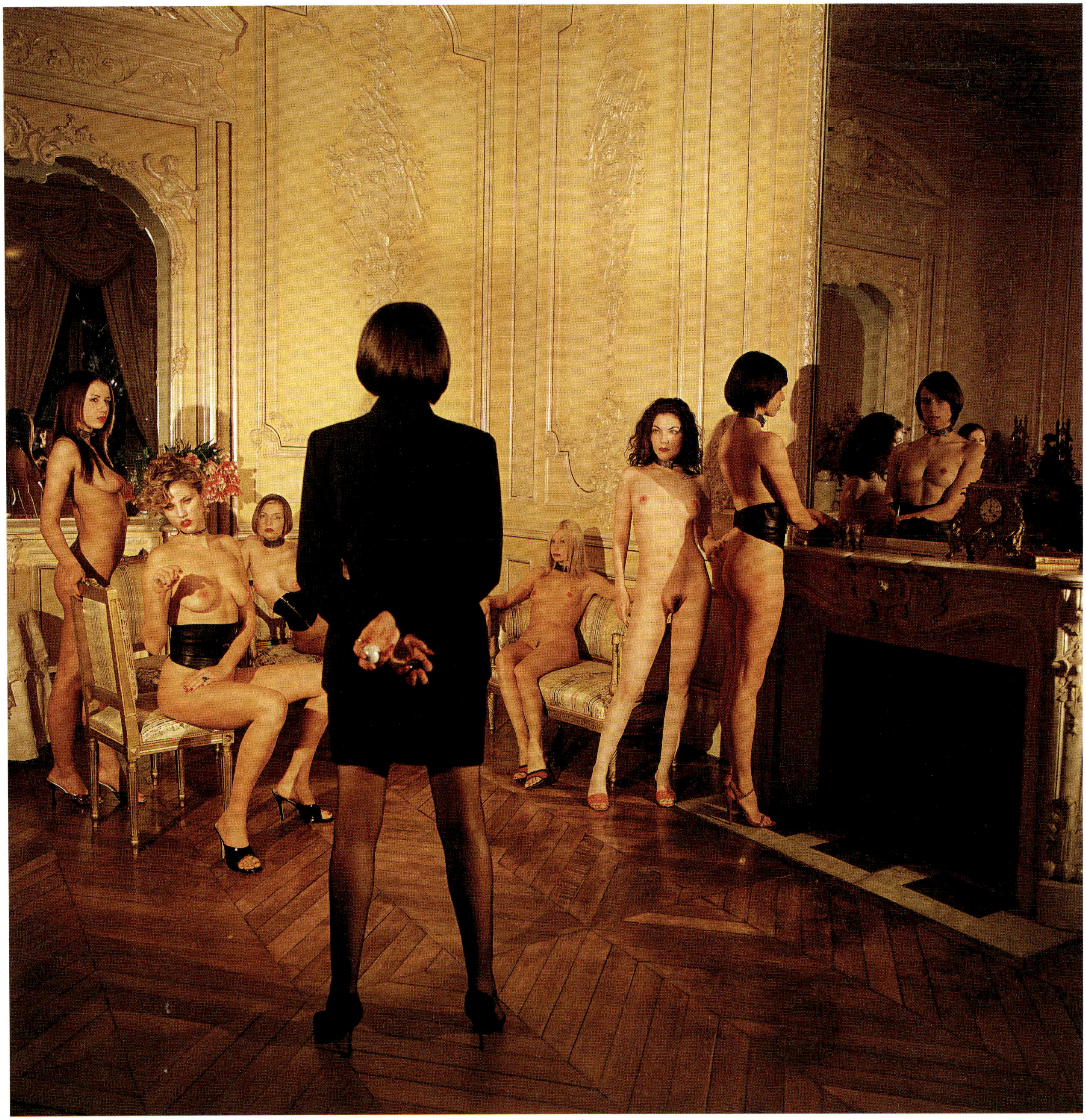

... Anne-Marie would bring out the token box. Each girl would take a token. Whoever drew the lowest number was then taken to the music room and arranged on the dais as O had been that first day. She then had to point to (save for O, who was exempted until her departure) Anne-Marie's right or left hand, in each of which she was holding a white or black ball. If she chose black, she was flogged; white, she was not. Anne-Marie never resorted to chicanery, even if chance condemned or spared the same girl several days in a row. Thus the torture of little Yvonne, who sobbed and cried out for her lover, was repeated four days running ...

... But how admirably suited to blows and irons was little Yvonne, how lovely it was to hear her moans and sighs, how lovely too to witness her body soaked with perspiration, and what a pleasure to wrest the moans and the sweat from her. For on two occasions Anne-Marie had handed O the thonged whip—both times the victim had been Yvonne—and told her to use it. The first time, for the first minute, she had hesitated, and at Yvonne's first scream O had recoiled and cringed, but as soon as had started in again and Yvonne's cries had echoed anew, she had been overwhelmed with a terrible feeling of pleasure ...

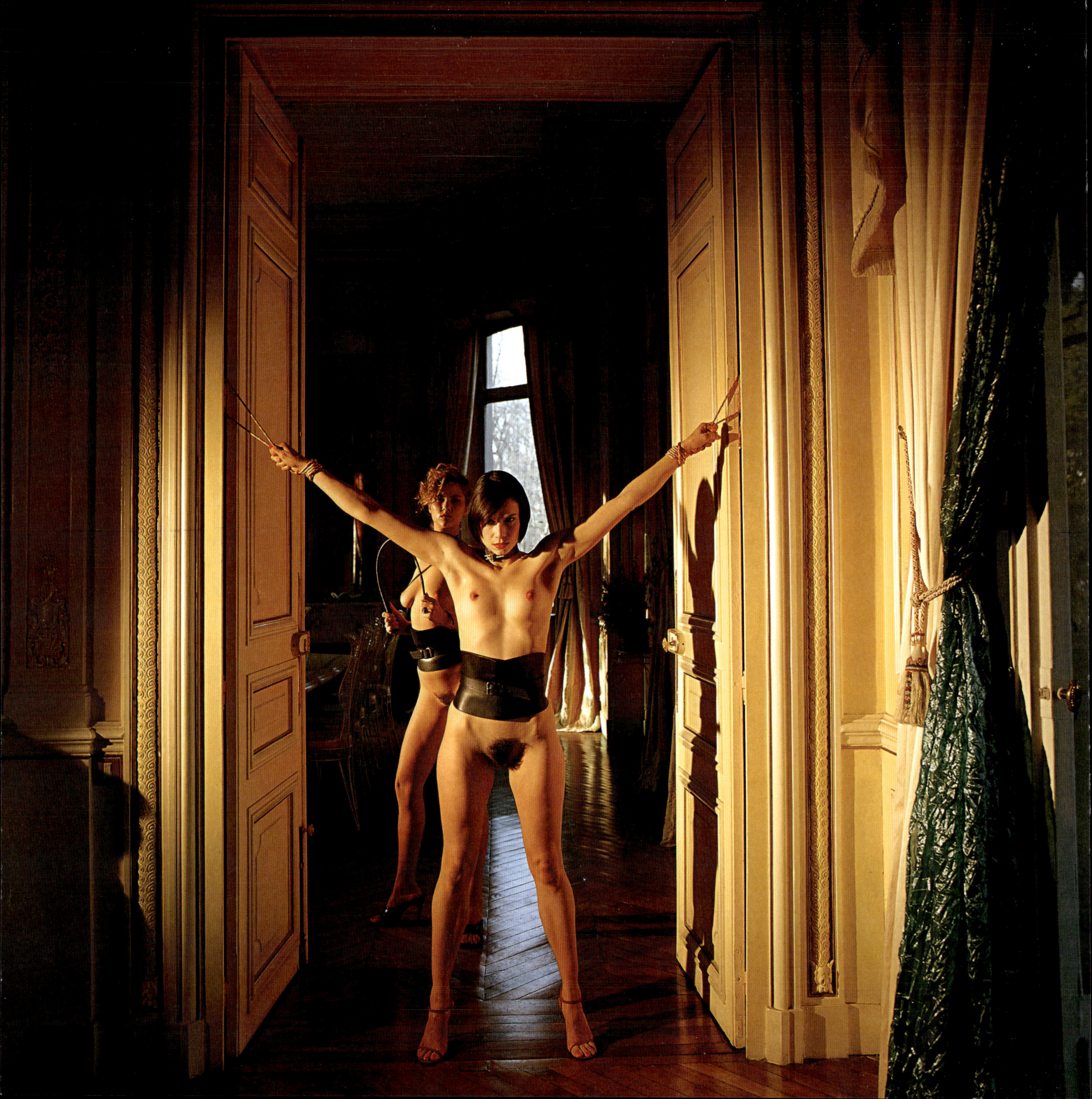

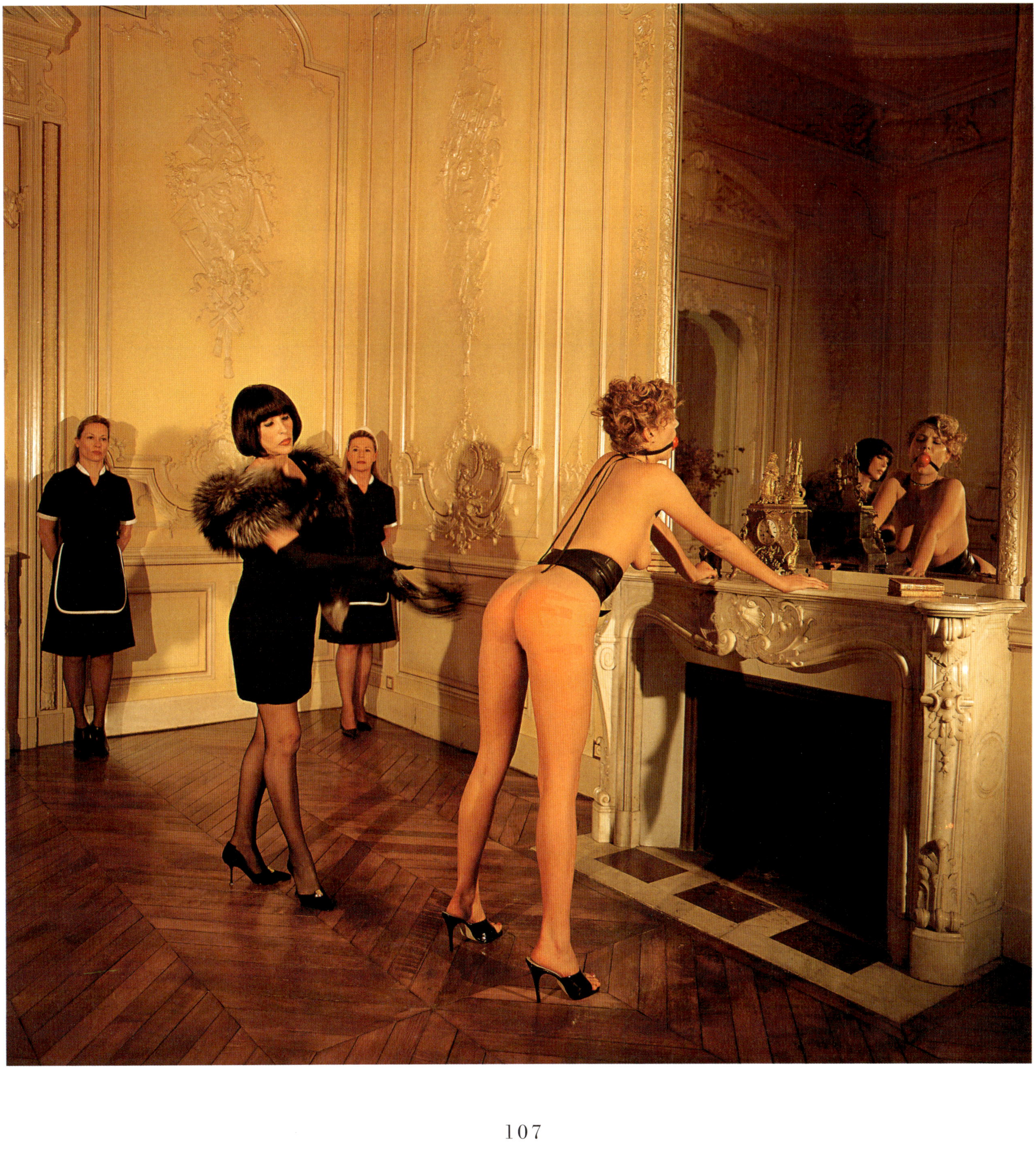

... No one possessed Anne-Marie. Anne-Marie demanded caresses without worrying about what the person giving them might feel, and she surrendered herself with an arrogant liberty. Yet she was all kindness and gentleness with O, kissed her on the mouth and kissed her breasts, and held her close against her for an hour before sending her back to her own room. She had removed her irons.

"These are your final hours here," she said, "you can sleep without the irons. The ones we'll put on you in a little while you'll never be able to take off."

She had run her hand softly, and at great length, over O's rear, then had taken her into the room where she, Anne-Marie, dressed, the only room in the house where there was a three-sided mirror. She had opened the mirror so that O could see herself.

"This is the last time you'll see yourself intact," she said. "Here, on this smooth, rounded area is where Sir Stephen's initials will be branded, on either side of the cleft in your behind." ...

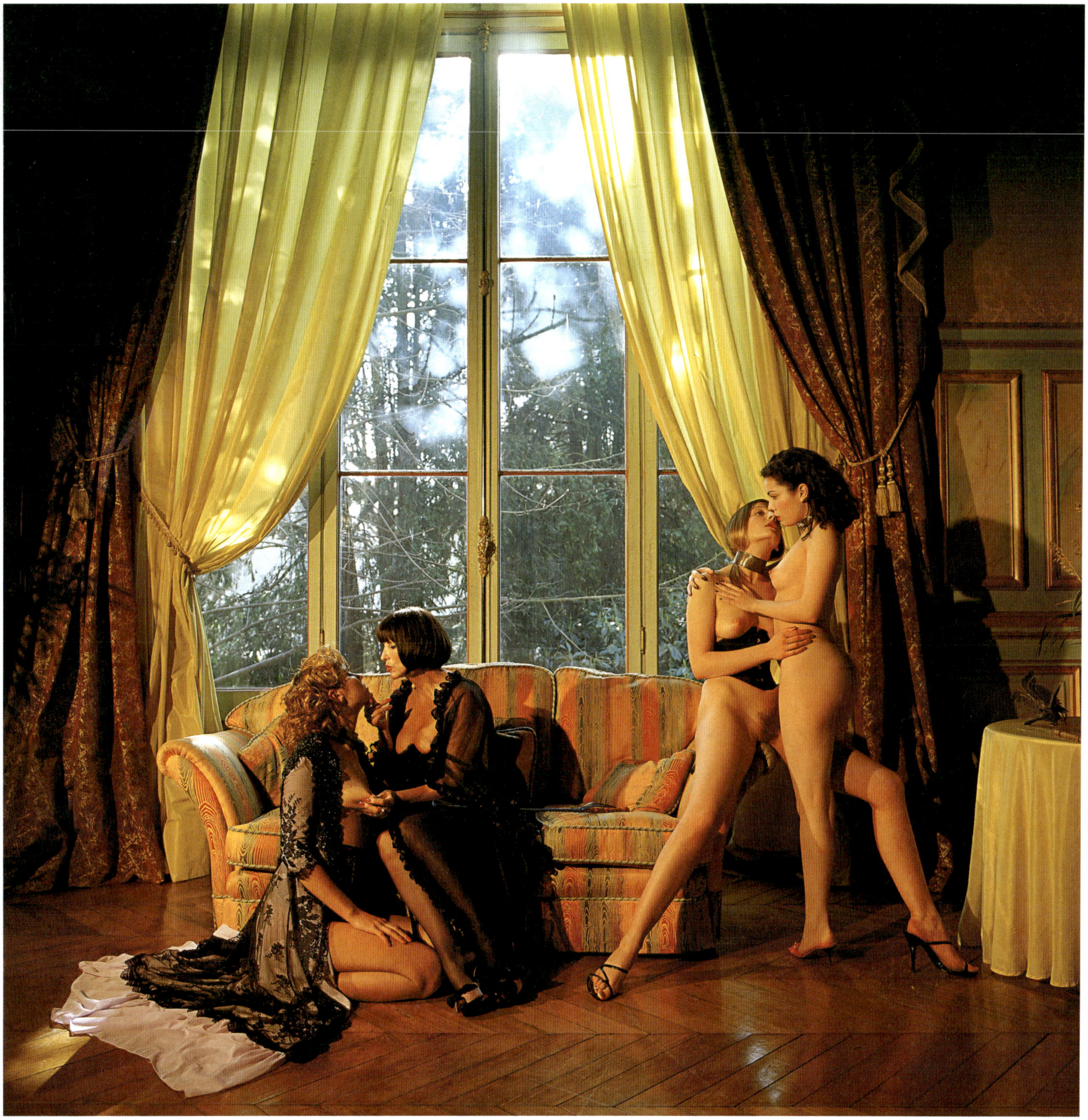

... Consumed by fear and terror, O felt one of Anne-Marie's hands on her buttocks, indicating the exact spot for the irons, she heard the hiss of a flame and, in total silence, heard the window being closed. She could have turned her head and looked, but she did not have the strength to. One single, frightful stab of pain coursed through her, made her go rigid in her bonds and wrenched a scream from her lips, and she never knew who it was who had, with both branding irons at once, seared the flesh of her buttocks, nor whose voice had counted slowly up to five, nor whose hand had given the signal to withdraw the irons.

When they unfastened her, she collapsed into Anne-Marie's arms and had time, before everything turned black around her and she completely lost consciousness, to catch a glimpse, between two waves of darkness, of Sir Stephen's ghastly pale face. ...

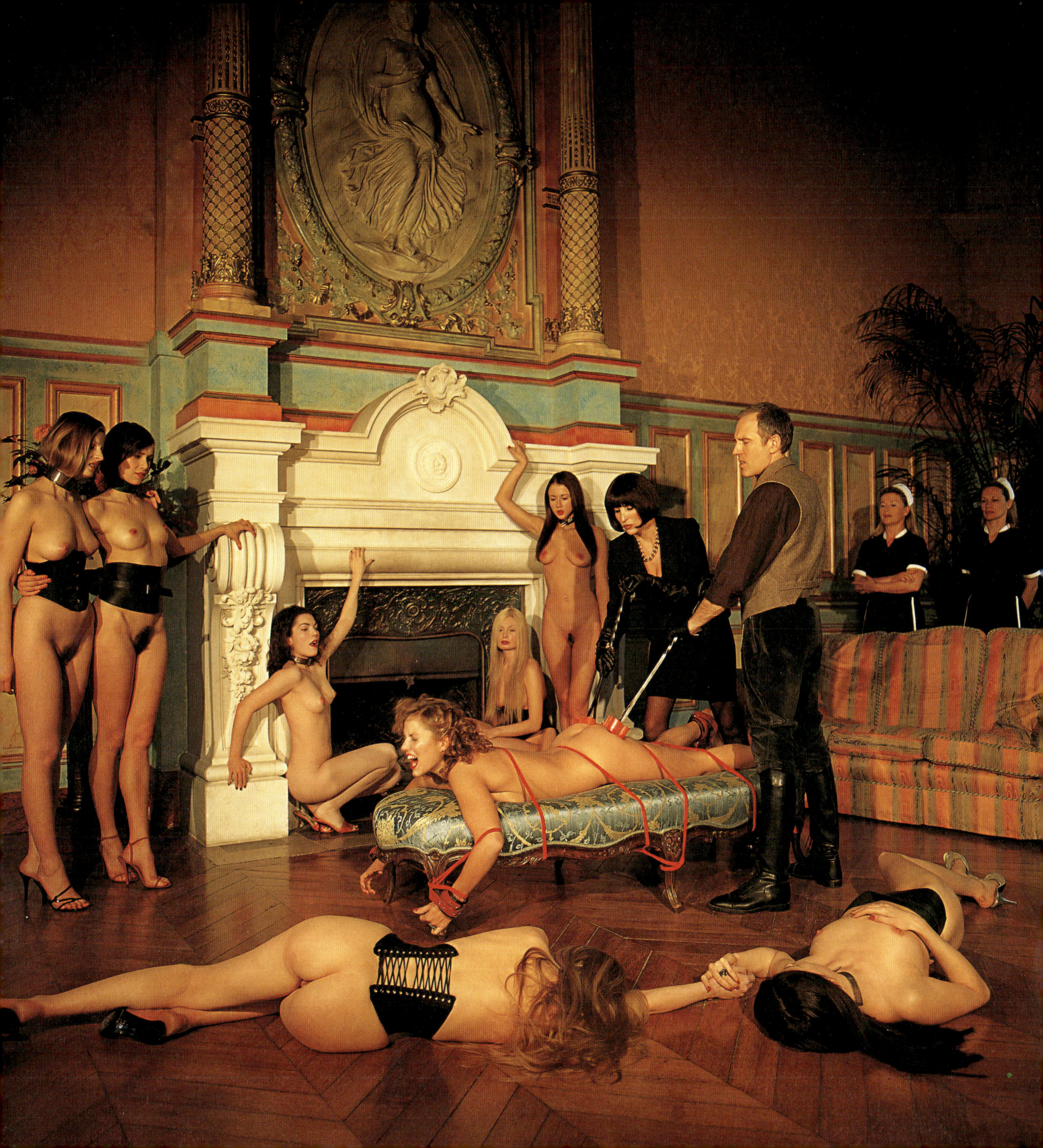

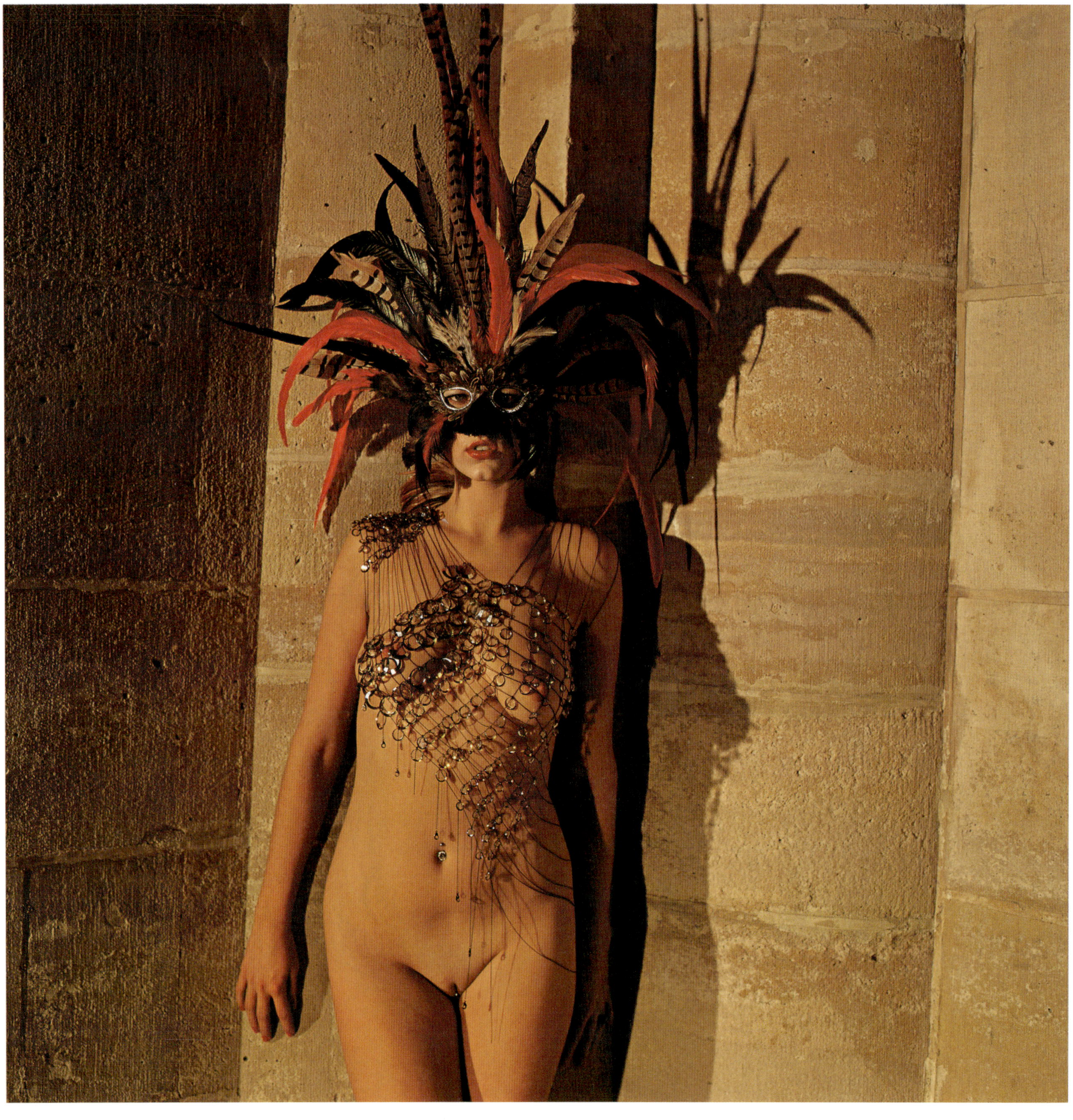

. . . In front of the full-length mirror, O tried on each of the masks. The most striking, and the one she thought transformed her most and was also the most natural, was one of the owl masks (there were two), no doubt because it was composed of tan and fawny feathers whose color blended beautifully with her tan; the cope of feathers almost completely concealed her shoulders, descending half way down her back and, in front, to the nascent curve of her breasts. Sir Stephen had her rub the lipstick from her lips, then said to her as he took off the mask:

"All right, you'll be an owl for the Commander. But O, and I hope you forgive me, you'll be taken on a leash." . . .

. . . The moon provided as much light as the candles, though, and when it fell upon O, who was being pulled forward by her little black shadow, Natalie, those who noticed her stopped dancing, and the men got to their feet. The boy near the record player, sensing that something was happening, turned around and, taken completely aback, stopped the record. O had come to a halt; Sir Stephen, motionless two steps behind her, was also waiting.

The Commander dispersed those who had gathered around O and had already called for torches to examine her more closely.

"Who is she," they were saying, "who does she belong to?"

"You, if you like," he replied . . .

114

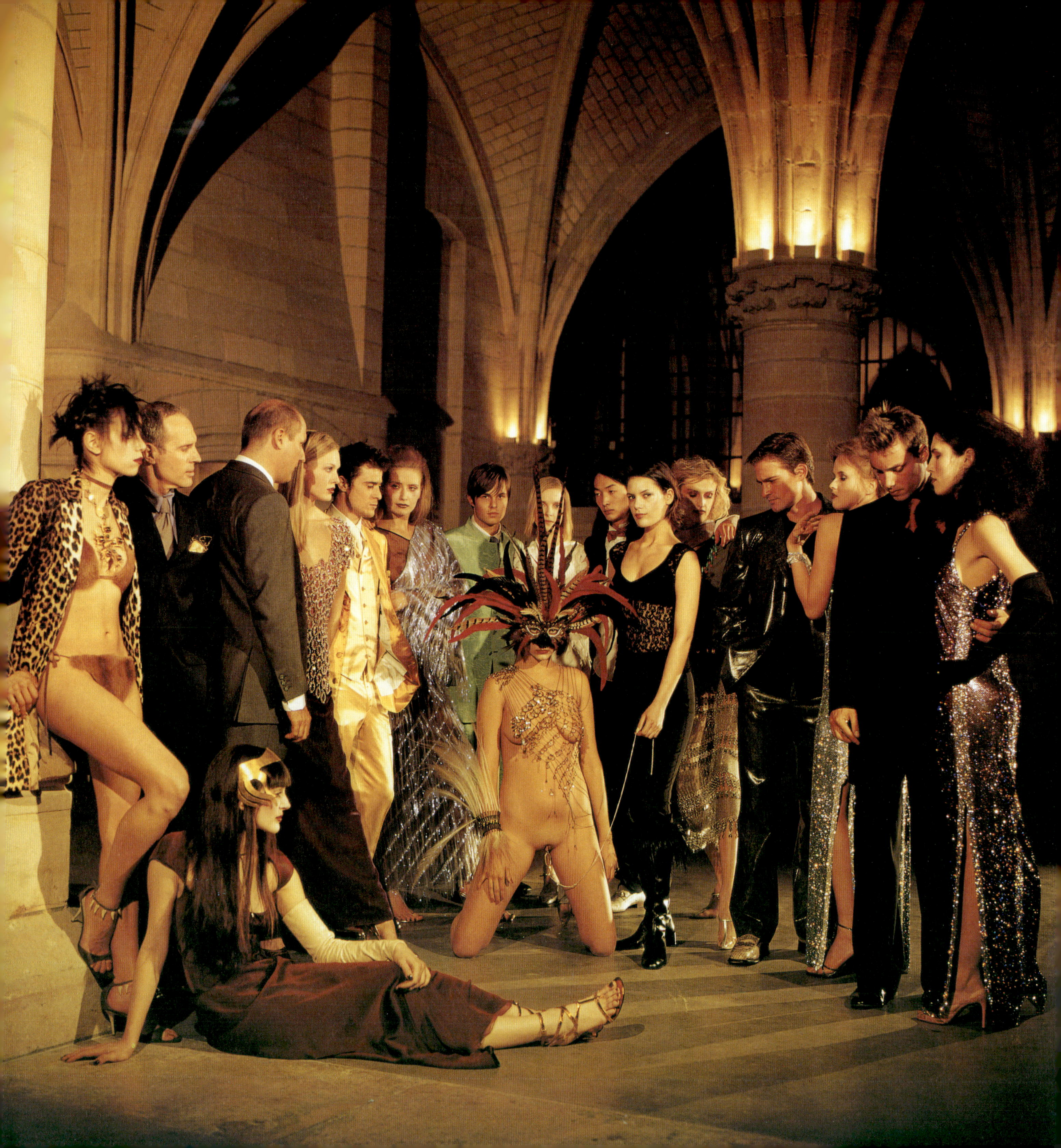

. . . O's eyes searched for Sir Stephen, and at first could not find him. Then she sensed his presence, reclining on a chaise longue at the other corner of the terrace. He was able to see her, she was reassured.

The music had begun again, the dancers were dancing again. As they danced, one or two couples moved over in her direction, as though by accident at first, then one of the couples dropped the pretense and, with the woman leading the way, marched boldly over. O stared at them with eyes that, beneath her plumage, were darkened with bister, eyes opened wide like the eyes of the nocturnal bird she was impersonating, and the illusion was so extraordinary that no one thought of questioning her, which would have been the most natural thing to do, as though she were a real owl, deaf to human language, and dumb.

From midnight till dawn, which began to lighten the eastern sky at about five, as the moon waned and descended toward the west, people came up to her several times, and some even touched her, they formed a circle around her several times and several times they parted her knees and lifted the chain, bringing with them one of those two-branched candlesticks of Provençal earthenware—and she could feel the flames from the candles warming the inside of her thighs—to see how she was attached. . . .

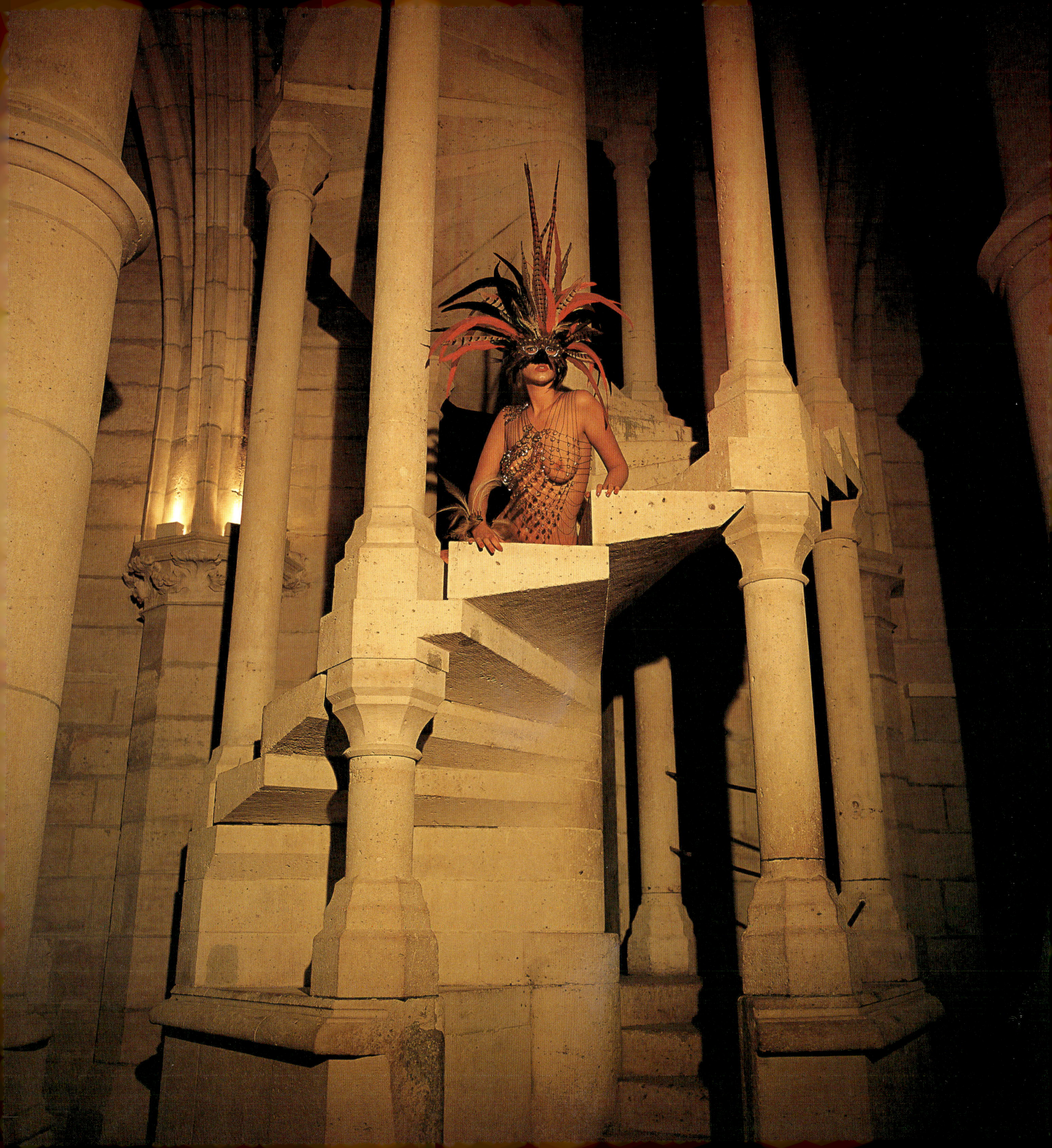

. . . It was only after daybreak, after all the dancers had left, that Sir Stephen and the Commander, awakening Natalie who was asleep at O's feet, helped O to her feet, led her to the middle of the courtyard, unfastened her chain and removed her mask and, laying her back upon a table, possessed her one after the other. . . .

ACKNOWLEDGMENTS

Concept and realization - Doris Kloster, *Production director* - Rory MacPherson, *Photography assistant* - Stéfanie Bertrand, *Production documentary photographer* - Eric Coubard, *Production assistant* - Jean-Paul Samoro, *Production accountant* - Mark Loveland, *Assistant to Doris Kloster* - Sabina Fogel, *Casting* - Doris Kloster, Susann Günther, Dominique Danesi, *Catering* - Fabienne Chastaing, *Make-up at Roissy, Anne-Marie's and ball scene* - Kenny Campbell, *Make-up assistant for ball scene* - Stéphanie Pracht, *Make-up at Sir Stephen's, O's apartment and photo studio* - Catherine Dargenton, *Hair* - Fouad, *Paris stylist* - Susann Günther, *New York costume production coordinator* - Anne Estes, *Corset dresses* - Margarita Caceres and Elkin Mann, NYC, from designs by Doris Kloster, *Purple robes and red cape* - Didier and Angelo, Paris, from designs by Doris Kloster, *Feather mask* - Doris Kloster, *Glass-beaded top and feather bracelet* - Eric Halley, Paris, *Jewelry at Roissy* - Hervé Ver der Straeten, Paris, *China* - L'Ancienne Manufacture Royale de Limoges, *Branding irons* - China Hamilton, London, *Whips and props* - From the private collection of Mistress Alexandra, Paris, *Bondage consultants* - Mastermind and Mistress Alexandra

---

Locations

Château de Saint-Loup, Charles-Henri de Bartillat, 79600 Saint-Loup, Lamairé
Tel (33) 5 49 64 81 73, Fax (33) 5 49 64 82 06, www.chateaudesaint-loup.com
Pages 2, 6, 10, 16, 18–64

Studio Zéro, Iñaki, 22, rue de la Folie-Méricourt, 75011 Paris
Tel (33) 1 43 55 77 56, Fax (33) 1 48 05 30 06
Pages 70, 73, 74

007 Productions, Valérie Chauris
Tel (33) 1 46 21 69 89, Fax (33) 1 46 21 79 71, Email connectim@007-production.com, www.007-production.com
Pages 79–87, 96–111

Model Agencies
Best One Models, Paris, Best Women, Paris, Roxanne Models, Paris, Supermodels, London, Rage, London

Thank you
Agie, Mistress Alexandra, Ralph Brancaccio, Patrice Catstyle, Étienne de Mailly, Kerrin Deisler, Tami Dituri, Gianni Panizza, Tracy Green, Heiner, Lisa Johnson, Julian Mongea, Lucien Loeb, Michèle and Mark, Christophe Mourthé, Catherine Miran and Valéric, Dominique - Noël Suret-Canale, Xavier Pelas, Alix Scialom, Carol and Gordon Spooner, Nadine Suret-Canale, Yannick

Special thanks
Paco Rabanne - Alexandre Boulais, Francesco Smalto - Patrick Alaux, Fifi Chachnil - Nawel, Sibilla Pavenstedt, Jean-Baptiste Rautureau - Tiphaine Macrez, Charles Jourdan and Yoichi Macasawa, Group 22V J-C. Chiroutte, Karin Arabian and Michel Vivier, Stéphane Saclier, Robert Beaulieu, Moschino, Carlos Puig Padilla, Rodolphe Menudier - Laurent, Suchel and Sandra, Stockings Sodibas - Yves Riquet www.Sodibas.com, John Ribbe - ISA, Eric Halley and Aigle - Girault-Totem, Christian Louboutin - Malou, Michel Perry - Quartier Général, Martin Sitbon and Jean Colonna, Michelle Montagne, Le Souk, Costume & Costumes, Chattoune, Orange Film, Première Heure, FGL Productions, Dominique Danesi, COMPOSIT - Rudi, Matphot - Marco, Fabio, Michèle and everyone at Chromatix Lab

Very special thanks
Olivia, Natasha, Donna, Adriane, Coreli, Snowwhite, Joanna, Salomé, Suzanna, Alexandra, Sébastien, Eric, Eric C, Jean-Pierre, Thorston, Klynt and Jean-Marc

---

Eddison Sadd Editions
Art Director - Elaine Partington
Mac Designer - Brazzle Atkins
Editorial Director - Ian Jackson
Editorial Assistance - Cecilia Walters
Translator (of Introduction) - Cecilia Walters
Production - Charles James and Karyn Claridge

Film processing
Chromatix Lab
3 rue des Trois-Bornes, 75011 Paris
Tel (33) 1 43 38 37 28
Fax (33) 1 40 21 33 48